Adopting Amish

Monica Marks

Published by Trellis Publishing, 2021.

This is a work of fiction. Similarities to real people, places, or events are entirely coincidental.

ADOPTING AMISH

First edition. July 1, 2021.

Copyright © 2021 Monica Marks.

ISBN: 979-8215413531

Written by Monica Marks.

ADOPTING AMISH

MONICA MARKS

Celia took a long drag of her cigarette and laughed as her friend fell off the table and crashed to the floor at her feet, his face contorted into a twisted, drunken smirk.

"Is that how you dance on the table, Kyle?" she scoffed, handing him the half-smoked butt in her hand. "Let me show you how it's done."

She rose, teetering on her high heels and climbed onto the picnic table as the group cheered her on.

"Celia! Celia! Celia!"

Grinning, she balanced herself on the rotting wood and began to bounce along to the loud dance music piping out of Meredith's iPhone.

The buzz from the beers she had drunk over the past hours was hitting her deliciously and she closed her grey eyes, swaying romantically to the music as if the gentle wind was her lover.

Her friends, hooted at the display but the moment was short lived as Meredith groaned loudly.

"Damn!" she cursed. "It's almost two o'clock!"

Celia's eyes flew open and she gaped at her best friend in disbelief.

"What?" she gasped, leaping off the surface and onto the grass, snatching up her own phone. She was intoxicated enough not to fully feel the surge of pain in her ankle as it fell to the side in her unceremonious landing.

She echoed Meredith's curse as she realized she had ten missed calls, all from the house phone.

"I am in such crap," Celia muttered, snatching her purse off the bench. "We have to get out of here."

"Me too," Meredith muttered. "My mom warned me that the next time I was late, she was taking the car away."

They barely said goodbye to the others as they rushed to Meredith's Honda Civic parked in the lot next to the park.

Celia dug through her purse for a piece of gum, chomping on it wildly to cover the smell of the alcohol on her breath.

"You're okay to drive?" Celia asked but it didn't really matter what the answer was; she was going to get in the car with her friend anyway. They didn't have time to worry about sobriety. Their parents were going to murder them both when they got home if they made it home alive.

"Maybe we should just sleep in my car," Mer suggested, checking her rear view nervously before she backed out. "Tell them that we stayed at Janey's."

"It's took late," Celia replied, glancing at her phone as it began to ring again. As if mimicking her cell, Meredith's also began to chime. She immediately silenced it as if to quiet her own conscience.

"Unbelievable," Meredith snapped. "They treat us like we're babies. A curfew, really?"

"Don't get me started," Celia muttered as they flew through the sleeping streets of Syracuse. Piles of garbage were on the curb for pick-up in the morning while the street vermin eyed the bags, waiting for their chance to rip them apart.

"We need to get our own place," Celia sighed.

Meredith nodded in agreement but they both knew it was a pipe dream. After all, they had only just graduated high school the previous year and sat in the limbo of what they wanted to do with their lives.

Neither had jobs nor did they have plans for college. They had spent the past months partying and trying to figure out their futures.

And it was difficult to leave home without any money.

"Text me tomorrow and let me know how it went," Meredith ordered as she pulled up to the two-storey house on Dickerson Street.

Celia sighed and nodded, reluctantly climbing from the passenger seat.

"If they haven't taken my phone," she agreed ruefully.

The porch lights were on, as were the ones in the living room but that was no surprise; Celia could never sneak into the house undetected.

They treat me like a twelve-year-old, she thought angrily.

As Meredith zoomed away, Celia saw her mother's face peer out from behind the lace curtains and even from the distance between them, the girl could read the relief on Christine Ryder's face.

Celia made her way up the walkway and realized she was slightly unsteady on her feet.

How many beers did I have? She asked herself as the front door flew open and she stood facing her furious parents.

"Where in God's name have you been?" Christine demanded as Celia brushed past her, hoping they could not smell the beer on her breath.

"I lost track of time," she mumbled, heading toward the stairwell. "Sorry."

"Sorry?" she screeched. "Where are you going, Celia? I'm talking to you!"

"I'm tired," she replied sullenly. "I'm going to bed."

"*You're tired*?" her mother echoed again. "You mean you're drunk, don't you? And have you been smoking? You reek like a bingo hall!"

"No!" she denied hotly but her mother was not letting her off the hook.

"It's bad enough that you're out God knows where, doing God knows what with God knows who until all hours of the morning but you lie too! I've had just about enough of this, Celia. Things are going to change around here!"

"Okay," she retorted. "Whatever you say, mother."

"Don't speak to your mom like that!"

Her father piped in for the first time, his dark eyes blazing with anger.

"I didn't say anything," she argued. "I'm agreeing!"

She smirked at her parents through hazy eyes and stifled a yawn.

It was the same old back and forth every night and she was getting tired of it.

"Go to bed," Earl said gruffly. "We'll talk in the morning."

Celia's smile widened, and she nodded as she saw she had won again.

"Sounds good," she replied smugly, turning to mount the stairs.

They are all talk all the time, she thought but before she opened the door to her bedroom, something made her stop in her tracks.

It was as if she had been held back by an invisible hand but for some reason, she paused in the hallway, out of view of her parents standing in the foyer.

"This is not normal behavior for a girl her age," Christine muttered to her father. "She's an adult and needs to start acting like one!"

"Unfortunately, it is normal," he replied but the annoyance in his voice was clear. "She will come around – eventually."

"I can't do this anymore, Earl. I thought with her background that she would be an easy child but since the day we brought her home..."

"It hasn't been all bad," her father said but there was uncertainty in his voice.

Brought me home? Celia thought, her dark eyebrows knitting in confusion. *What does that mean? From the hospital?*

"I think that it's time to send her out in the world," Christine continued, the aggravation in her voice clear. "I'm done with coddling her, Earl. We'll tell her the truth about her birth tomorrow and maybe she can go on a quest to find her real family."

"Christine! What a thing to say!" The shock in her father's voice was clear but it was nothing compared to the stunning blow which Celia had been delivered.

"You don't think it's a good idea?" Christine scoffed. "When she finds out that she comes from Amish roots, she'll realize how good she has it and come running home, begging for forgiveness!"

"Or she'll stay away forever. Is that what you want, Christine?"

Her mother snorted derisively.

"Celia can't go four hours without her hair straightener. You think she's going to adapt to the life?"

Her father was silent, but Celia's heart was pounding so hard, she was sure they could hear it from the bottom of the stairs.

What are they saying?

She slumped against the wall of the hallway, her mind whirling as she tried to process what she had just learned.

Am I adopted?

Any tiredness which had plagued Celia upon her arrival home dissolved the moment she heard her parents' conversation.

She retreated to her bedroom, her pulse racing as she tried to collect herself, pain filling her heart.

They lied to me for almost twenty years? She thought, horrified at the realization. *Why would they keep that from me?*

Celia did not know which was more hurtful; the fact that they had hidden the truth from her or the fact that her mother wanted her to leave.

Am I that bad? She wondered but as she thought it, she envisioned herself grinning mockingly at her concerned mother.

A flood of shame washed over her as she thought about how difficult she had been over the years to her parents.

She had never tried in school or made any effort to help around the house. She was argumentative and broke any rules her mother and father laid out for her.

But she had to ask herself if she had acted that way because she had always secretly known she did not belong in the two storey Tudor house where she had been raised.

Maybe she never really loved me because I wasn't her real child, she thought, tears welling in her slate grey eyes. *Am I really Amish?*

She sat up in her darkened room and listened for signs of life in the house.

There was not a peep to be heard as Celia slipped out of the bedroom and stole down the stairs toward her father's study at the back of the main floor.

If there were adoption papers, they would be in with her father's file, undoubtedly and without hesitation, Celia entered the dark paneled room, swallowing her tears.

She flicked on the desk lamp and pulled open drawers, rifling through the paperwork without regard for keeping it in order.

Even if she knew what she was looking for exactly, she wouldn't know where to start.

But it didn't take long to locate the records at the back of one of Earl's filing cabinets, tucked away out of sight.

It was labeled "Celia" and she knew what it was before looking inside the manila folder.

With trembling hands, she pried it open and her hand flew to her mouth as she was faced with the reality of what she had overheard earlier.

She poured over the original birth certificate, the lump in her throat almost choking her as she read.

The date of birth and first name were the only things she knew to be true. Everything else was a shock.

I was born in Massena, New York to a woman named Anna Bechler.

Behind the birth certificate was one of adoption, declaring Earl and Christine Ryder as her parents, six months after she was born.

Celia turned to the computer and logged in, pulling up Google as fast as her fingers would allow.

She typed "Massena, New York" and watched as her search took her to an Amish community in St. Lawrence County.

Celia fell back against the high back leather chair, shaking her head in disbelief.

Slowly, she rose to her feet without returning the files to their place, the den depicting the same disorganization she felt in her soul.

She wanted her parents to know that she finally saw the truth.

If they want me gone, gone I will be.

Massena was a small town on the Canadian border, banking on the Grass and St. Lawrence Rivers.

There was a quaint, peaceful beauty about it, a rustic feel which Syracuse lacked and despite her resolve to be unimpressed, Celia found herself enchanted with the easy going pace of her surroundings.

She was at a loss of where to start her search for her birth mother, but the three-hour bus trip north had given her time to think.

I can start at the hospital where the certificate was issued, she reasoned. It seemed a good a place as any.

She arrived at Massena Memorial Hospital mid-morning but when she spoke to the woman at the inquiries desk, Celia was met with news she had not anticipated.

"I'm sorry, honey," the stern-looking receptionist told her. "But that is not any information me or anyone else in this hospital could provide you with."

"Why?" Celia asked in disbelief. "I'm looking for my mother!"

"I understand, hon," she said. "But even if those records weren't sealed, I am forbidden to give out information about patient care."

There was a glimmer of pity in her pinched face, but sympathy was not what Celia needed; she needed answers.

Celia opened her mouth to protest but she could tell that arguing would get her nowhere.

It's not her fault she can't help me, she thought miserably, turning away. *She's only doing her job.*

The understanding did nothing to alleviate her mounting frustration and she impulsively touched her coat pocket for her cell phone.

I should call Meredith and tell her what happened, she thought but immediately she shook her head, grunting in annoyance.

In her anger, she had fled into the night with a packed knapsack and her bank card, but she had purposely left her cell behind for her parents to find.

I wanted them to suffer but instead, I am the one without. Not smart, Celia. You are acting like an impulsive brat. Maybe mom was right about you.

Shoving the thought of her disloyal parents aside, Celia tossed her hair over her shoulder and looked about for a payphone.

Suddenly she was regretting her actions.

I shouldn't have come in the middle of the night like this. I should have planned this better.

But it was too late for second thoughts; she was there, and she was going to find her mother, Anna Bechler no matter what.

The alternative was to do as Christine anticipated; return to Syracuse with her tail between her legs, begging for forgiveness.

I have nothing to beg for, she thought hotly. *They lied to me. I did nothing wrong.*

But a nagging in the back of her mind told her that she had been anything but an ideal daughter to her adoptive parents.

She silenced it again and started toward the main entrance.

Minimally, she had to call Meredith and let her know she was okay.

The thought of hearing her best friend's voice cheered her up slightly.

Who knows? She might even have some sage advice for me.

But as she approached the glass doors leading outside, her attention was diverted from the payphones in the vestibule to the parking lot just beyond her view.

Two middle aged Amish men stood near a horse and cart, chatting as they boarded the bench.

Before she could stop herself, Celia bolted outside and ran toward them, her mind whirling.

"Excuse me!" she gasped, reaching them as one man reached for the reins.

He peered at her somewhat warily with dark eyes.

The men exchanged a glance and the passenger stroked his long beard and shifted his eyes downward.

"*Ja?*"

"I'm looking for a woman named Anna Bechler. Do you know her?"

An almost frozen silence seemed to hang in the air as the dark eyed man studied her face.

"I do not," he finally said and before Celia could ask anything else, he nodded and set away from the parking lot.

Suddenly Celia was embarrassed. She wished she had not acted so impulsively but she was running out of ideas.

You can't just run around asking random Amish men if they know your birth mother, she chided herself. *What were you thinking?*

Behind her, she heard a chuckle and she spun to see an attractive man watching her, his arms folded over his chest as he grinned at her.

"What are you laughing at?" she demanded, inadvertently looking him over.

His bright blue eyes sparkled with amusement as he swept his long, dark blonde hair aside to return her stare.

"You don't know much about the Amish, do you?" he asked, lazily, his beam widening.

"And you do?" she demanded hotly, noting his jeans and t-shirt.

He certainly didn't seem to have an Anabaptist bone in his lean but muscular physique.

But he might be local and be able to help me with my search. Maybe he can find me an "in" to the community.

"I know enough to know that you can't corner them and ask them about their congregants like you just did."

Celia gritted her teeth and bit back the urge to retort at the almost arrogant young man.

"Thank you for the advice," she replied tightly. "Do you have another way I might be able to find someone I'm looking for?"

He cocked his head to the side and stared at her for a long moment.

"There is a Bechler family I know of," he finally said, and Celia's head jerked up to gape at him.

"You know some of the Amish families?" she asked hopefully, and he howled as if she had asked the funniest question.

"Yes," he replied, laughing. "Some."

"Is there an Anna Bechler? She would be older than us."

He shook his head and uncrossed his arms, scuffing his toe against the pavement as if trying to remove a spot.

"No," he replied quietly. "There is no one I know by that name."

Disappointment seized Celia again and she began to feel as if the wind was knocked out of her.

"Why are you looking for this woman?" he asked.

Celia stared at him stonily.

"That's none of your business," she replied shortly, turning away but to her surprise, he reached out to grab her arm.

"Wait a moment," he said and for the first time, she noticed he had a peculiar accent, not unlike the man she had just spoken with at the cart. "Maybe I can still help you."

His touch sent an unexpected flood of comfort through her and she realized that she was being rude for no reason.

I could certainly use a friend in this town, she thought, turning to answer but as she parted her lips, her brow furrowed.

A small group was fast approaching them, two girls and a boy, all in homespun clothes. The girls wore prayer bonnets over their braids and Celia instantly identified them as Amish.

"Levi! We have been searching everywhere for you!" one blonde girl exclaimed, eyeing them with suspicion. "We must get back to the district."

Slowly, he pivoted, releasing his hold on Celia's arm.

"I have been right here," he replied easily. "How is John?"

"His ankle is broken. We have to inform his father," the girl said but her green eyes were fixated on Celia. "Who is this?"

Levi shrugged his shoulders.

"I have no idea," he said, a smile toying on his lips. "She hasn't told me her name yet."

Celia gaped at him in disbelief.

"You're Amish?" she finally managed to gasp, and he nodded.

"You did not know?" Levi said innocently.

Celia felt a hot flush rising to her cheeks and she wondered if she was going to be met with humiliation at every turn.

Without responding, she began to walk away.

"Wait!" he called out again, hurrying after her but she didn't stop.

"Levi!" his friends yelled after him, but the young man continued to follow Celia as she headed back toward the payphones.

This was a mistake. I'm going to call Meredith and -

"Come back to the district with us," Levi said as he caught up with her. "I will bring you to the Bechler house and you can ask them about Anna."

She paused mid-step and peered at him warily.

"You can do that?" she asked uncertainly, her gaze shifting toward the group at his back. He laughed.

"Why not?"

Celia did not have an answer and she stood, trying to decide what to do.

"Or you can run around asking any Amish person you see about Anna Bechler," he suggested.

Celia made up her mind, choosing to ignore his jesting tone.

"All right," she agreed slowly. "I'll go with you."

He shook his head.

"Not so fast," he replied, holding up his hand and Celia felt a pang of anger course through her.

"Is this a game to you?" she asked furiously. "Because this is my life!"

His blue eyes widened in surprise and he shook his head.

"No," he answered quietly. "It is not a game. I only wanted to know your name."

A hot blush stained her cheeks and she gazed at her hands in contrition.

"Sorry," she mumbled. "It's Celia. Celia Ryder."

"Well Celia Ryder, I am Levi Miller."

He held out a calloused hand and she accepted it tentatively, raising her head to meet his vivid eyes.

"Come on," he said gently, holding her palm a moment longer than necessary. "Let's find your friend."

The ride to the district was decidedly uncomfortable.

Levi, Celia and the blonde were crammed into one cart while the other two took another.

The girl's name was Eva and she was Levi's younger sister. It quickly became apparent that she was highly suspicious of Celia, despite her brother's explanation.

"Why are you looking for this woman?" Eva asked curtly. "You do not look like someone who knows many Amish people."

"I don't know any Amish people," Celia agreed but she offered no more as Levi cast her a sly look.

He gave her a brief sense of security in the confusion sweeping through her and she was grateful he had approached her, even though Eva's disapproval was apparent.

"Why aren't you wearing...I mean, where are your suspenders and hat?" Celia heard herself asking Levi, hoping to shift the focus off herself. The question sounded ridiculous when she voiced it but there was no way to take it back.

Eva scowled and muttered something under her breath.

"We are experiencing *Rumspringa*," Levi told her, but he could easily read that she had no idea what he was talking about.

"As Anabaptists, we are afforded the option of being baptized when we come of age. Our traditions dictate that we go into the English world and experience what we will be forsaking if we are to accept the *Ordnung* and be baptized," Levi explained. "Some of us choose to wear Englisch clothes and partake in activities usually reserved for the Englisch."

"That isn't frowned upon?" Celia asked in disbelief.

"Not at all. It is expected. We must be certain that we are content with our decision to renounce the outside world before pledging ourselves to the community and God."

Celia was quiet, but she studied his profile curiously.

"Do a lot of people choose not to become baptized after *Rumspringa*?" she asked. To her shock, he shook his head.

"Very, very few," he replied. "Our ways offer a sense of community and support that people in the English world cannot appreciate fully. Even those who stray for a time tend to find their way home."

He speaks with so much pride about his culture. I wonder what it's like to have such an affection about where you come from.

Guiltily, Celia thought of the days she had spent partying and disrespecting her parents.

What would it be like if I had an entire congregation of people backing me, rooting for me, ensuring I didn't fall? she wondered.

The thought was inane...wasn't it?

You could never live without electricity or indoor plumbing, she thought, shaking her head.

Yet she couldn't help but envision what life would be like, living in such a beautiful environment, surrounded by like-minded people.

Your birth mother was Amish. You could have grown up this way.

It was almost an hour before Levi pulled the wagon up a path leading toward a large, well-kept farmhouse in the distance.

"Levi, you cannot simply bring her to the Bechlers like this," Eva protested suddenly as they neared the building.

"Well I would call if I could," Celia piped up, but Eva did not find her joke amusing although her brother did cast her a quick grin.

"What harm can it do?" Levi replied, stopping the wagon at the front of the house. "She is only looking for information, not inviting herself to move in."

Eva's frown deepened but she only pursed her lips as Celia slowly slid herself onto the ground.

"Go on," Levi encouraged, and she realized that he was not going with her.

"You're staying here?" she demanded, her face growing pale.

He seemed surprised.

"You want me to come with you?"

"Yes!" she cried before she could stop herself. She gazed at him helplessly.

"Yes, please," she added, and he shrugged nonchalantly, jumping down to join her.

"Don't take too long!" Eva snapped. "We still have chores to do this evening and I would like to get word on John."

Levi paused and glanced at his sister.

"Take the wagon and go home. I'll walk."

"And what about her?" Eva wanted to know. "She can't walk back to town!"

"I can take Celia back to Massena after supper. Tell *Mammi* and *Daed* I am bringing home a guest. Oh! But do not tell them she is Englisch. I want to see their reaction."

"Levi!" Eva called horrified, but he grabbed Celia's arm and led her toward the house.

"She doesn't like me," Celia muttered, peering back over her shoulder as Eva glowered at her.

"She does not know you," he replied as they climbed the spotless steps onto the whitewashed porch. "And she is wary of outsiders. It is not uncommon to see that."

"You don't know me either," Celia reminded him. "And you're being very kind to me."

A now-familiar smile formulated on Levi's lips.

"Maybe my reasons are a little bit selfish," he confessed quietly. "But I think you are the most beautiful girl I have ever seen."

The confession sent a jolt of heat through her.

"Oh," she mumbled, unsure of what else to say.

What can I tell him? I think you're gorgeous too but you're Amish and I'm looking for my birth mother, so this could never work? I want to learn more about your world because I feel unexplainably safe here, but your people won't accept me because I'm an outsider?

Levi stepped forward to save her from saying anymore, knocking loudly on the front door but he maintained the beam on his face as if he understood her thoughts somehow.

"Levi Miller! What are you doing here?" An older woman answered the door, wiping her weathered hands on her apron as she pushed the screen outward.

Levi stepped aside.

"*Guder nammidaag*, Eliza. Is David home?" he asked her, and Celia was surprised to hear him calling her by her first name.

"*Ja*," she replied but her eyes rested on Celia, her smile fading slightly. "Who is this?"

"This is Celia," he volunteered. "She is looking for a friend of hers."

"A friend?" Eliza echoed, her grey eyes narrowing slightly. "Which friend would that be?"

"Levi!" a man cried, appearing in the foyer. "What brings you here?"

"Hello, David. This is my friend, Celia Ryder. She is looking for someone and I told her you might know where to find her."

"I know who you are!" Eliza growled angrily, stepping toward Celia. "You are not welcome here."

Celia's eyes widened in shock.

"Me?" she asked in confusion. "How do you know who I am? I've never been here before!"

"*Mammi*, what a thing to say!" David said, his face contorting in embarrassment. He turned to Celia apologetically.

"Forgive my mother," he said, joining them on the porch. "Who are you looking for, Miss Ryder and why do you believe I can help?"

"I am looking for a woman named Anna Bechler," Celia said slowly, aware of the scathing look which Eliza Bechler gave her.

David's face turned opaque as his mother grunted.

"You think I do not know you are Anna's illegitimate child?" Eliza screeched. "I would recognize those sinful eyes anywhere. You are not welcome here after how your mother has disgraced this family. Go away now and do not come back!"

Celia's cheeks turned crimson but suddenly she saw that Eliza's own irises were colored identically to hers.

She is related to me! She is related to Anna too!

"I'm sorry," she whispered, looking helplessly at Levi who appeared as confused as Celia. "I don't know anything about her. I am trying to find her."

"Are you pretending you are not her child?" Eliza snapped but David interjected before Celia could answer.

"*Mammi,* go inside and wait, please. I would like to speak with Celia alone."

"Provided you send her on her way, David!" Eliza snarled.

"I will," David said quickly. He ushered the old woman into the house, leaving Levi and Celia to stare at one another, dumbfounded.

"What was that all about?" she whispered, dread clutching her heart. "It sounds like my mother was hated here!"

"She may have been excommunicated from the church," Levi muttered as if trying to reconcile what was happening.

"You mean, like, shunned?" Celia gasped, the blood draining from her face. She did not know much about Amish culture, but she knew a little bit about shunning from what she had read.

"If that's true, I must be slapping them in the face by coming here. We should go, Levi!"

She turned to hurry away before David could return but Levi blocked her way.

"Are you Anna Bechler's daughter?" he asked, his voice thick with confusion. Miserably, Celia nodded.

"I believe so. I – I was adopted when I was six months old. I only learned recently about any of this!"

Recently like yesterday, she thought, swallowing the rock in her throat.

"We should go," she said again, trying to pass him but as she moved, David reappeared on the porch.

"My apologies," he said again. "Please come and sit down, Celia."

She shook her head.

"No," she told him firmly, willing the tears in her eyes not to slip down her cheeks. "I am leaving. I'm sorry – I didn't know anything about this."

"I know you did not. How could you? You were adopted before you were a year old."

Celia froze.

"You know I about my adoption?" she whispered, her mind racing.

David sighed deeply and gestured for her to sit on one of the wicker pieces on the wraparound porch.

"Please, let me explain."

Reluctantly, she sank onto the edge of a seat and Levi perched beside her, their stares fixated on David's woeful expression.

He nervously stroked the hairs on his face before inhaling sharply.

"Your mother was a willful, stubborn girl," he began. "She was the youngest and the most headstrong of six children. She was engaged to marry a man name Jethro Schmidt the year following her baptism, but both the betrothal and the baptism were not her choice. As you can see, my mother can be quite sharp tongued and when it came to Anna, she was tenfold worse."

"Your mother..." Celia trailed off, her thoughts spinning too wildly for her to catch. "Your mother is Anna's mother?"

"Yes," David offered. "My mother is your grandmother and I am your *onkle*."

He smiled weakly, but it did not meet his eyes and he avoided her gaze as he continued his story.

"Anna had a romance with the Englisch world, even after *Rumspringa*. It was no surprise that she eventually fell in love with an Englischer during her engagement. She tried to hide their trysts but when she was with child, with you, well, there was no way around it."

Celia's mouth parted but no words came out. She looked Levi, but his mouth had pursed into a fine line and she could not read his expression.

"Jethro Schmidt was furious and called off the wedding, of course but Anna was fine with that – she was going to live with her new love in Ottawa where he was from. My mother was furious, but Anna was in love and she disappeared that very night, despite my pleas that she stay. Even disgraced, the church would have helped her through and you would have been raised here with family as *Gotte* intended."

David paused to visibly gulp back the emotion in his throat and Celia felt a twinge in her heart.

He loves his sister so much.

"Why did she give me up?" Celia whispered but there was something in his eye, something which only added to her mounting apprehension.

"Anna was very sick, Celia. It was something she learned when she was pregnant, but she told no one, not until you were almost four months old and she could no longer care for herself. She managed to get a letter to me and I was shocked to learn she was not in Canada at all but in Rochester all along. Her lover had left her without a word, the same way she had left us. She reasoned that he had not signed on for both a sick wife and a new baby, but I think he had never intended to do right by her."

"Why didn't she come home?" Celia demanded, aghast by the story, realizing that the end was not what she had been hoping for.

"It would not have been a simple matter, Celia," David explained. "She knew she had been shunned. Anna had no choice but to struggle alone and unwell until she was forced to call on me."

Celia stared at him, the tears finally falling to her cheeks.

"I wanted to take you home with me," he told his niece tenderly and she could see the pain in his eyes. "But she made me swear that you would never be exposed to our mother's harsh tongue. She wanted you to be brought up Englisch at all costs."

The shame in his face was apparent.

"So, I arranged the adoption as Celia died of her cancer quietly a few months later."

With glistening eyes, he stared at her imploringly.

"I do not expect you to understand, Celia," he told her, and she could hear the shame in his tone, but Celia did understand.

"You did the right thing," she told her uncle and his mouth parted in surprise.

"You – you aren't angry?" he asked dubiously, and she shook her head vehemently.

"I have barely known your mother for two minutes and I can see why my mother would want to keep a child from her. What a horrible woman to reject her dying child and her own grandchild!"

A combination of fury and disgust grew inside Celia, but David shook his head.

"You do not understand," he sighed. "My mother doesn't know that Anna died."

"What?" Celia and Levi gasped in unison.

"I knew she would never forgive herself if I told her the truth," David mumbled but Celia could see that hearing the words aloud sounded heinous.

"You must tell her!" Levi growled, leaping to his feet. "She has lost out on the opportunity to make amends with Anna, but she can still know Celia. David, you must!"

He hung his head miserably.

"I know," he whispered. "I fight with myself every day about this. I think you coming here, Celia, is a sign from *Gotte* to finally do the right thing."

Laboriously, he rose and turned toward the house.

"Will you come with me?" he asked Celia quietly. "I feel that it will be better having you nearby to soften the shock of my words."

"Only if Levi can come too," she said, and David agreed.

Before Celia could follow her uncle, Levi captured her hand in his and spun her around to stare into her troubled eyes.

"David is right," Levi told her. "You being here is a sign from *Gotte*."

Despite the turmoil of emotions, Celia felt a smile forming on her lips, his words making her heart beat faster.

"Is it?" she replied. "How so?"

He chuckled.

"You cannot tell?" he asked.

Levi leaned in and kissed her cheek softly, brushing her dark hair away from her face.

"I imagine when you woke this morning, you did not envision being kissed by an Amish boy, did you?"

Celia laughed aloud.

"No," she conceded. "I did not expect anything that I found here."

The smiled faded from her lips but Levi continued to stare at her warmly.

"I am sorry about your mother," he said softly. "That is a devastating thing to learn."

But Celia shook her head, realizing that she had learned something very important on the whirlwind journey.

Whoever said you can't pick your family is wrong. Family is not about blood ties, it's about people who love you and carry you through the roughest time, no matter what happens. Family puts up with your bratty behavior and your tears.

"There is no need to be sorry," she replied. "My mother and my father are alive and well in Syracuse. Would you like to meet them?"

Levi squeezed her hand, his grin overtaking his face.

"Yes," he replied. "I would very much."

She returned his embrace and smile.

"Good. Because tomorrow I need to go home with my tail between my legs and apologize to them both."

EMMA'S QUIET AMISH TOWN

GILLIAN BROWN

Chapter 1

Emma stood on the front porch, looking out into the bleak distance. Her quiet Amish town had strict rules by which each member had to abide, and Emma was doing her best to be patient, but her frustration was mounting. It had been days now. *Where was he?*

Three days ago, Emma had sent an urgent letter to the Bishop, asking that he approve medical treatment at the English hospital nearby for her father who was worsening with each passing hour. She hadn't heard a word back. Yet, with each passing day her father's face grew more sallow and his spirit seemed to fade.

The once-vibrant farmer had been reduced to a mere shadow of his former self and Emma feared that he was dying.

When her Amish boyfriend Steve, had made the decision to leave her, things had reached a boiling point. Steve had been her father's right hand on the farm and all the work now fell to her father.

"I just don't think this is the will of Heavenly Father," Steve had said to her, holding back tears as he clutched a duffle bag in his hand. "So, are you leaving the Amish or are you just leaving me?" Emma had fired back. Steve had balled his hands into tight fists. "There's more to life than this, Emma!" Steve had screamed at her. His rage was a stark contrast to his usually calm demeanor. Steve had always wanted more than she was willing to give. He'd wanted her to be his wife, but before that, he'd wanted her to make love to him, and Emma had refused.

"What's wrong with you? All the Amish girls do it." Steve had pleaded, after calling her a prude. "It doesn't feel right," Emma had said softly. "Why doesn't it feel right?" Steve had demanded. "Because I don't love you," Emma said in a whisper.

After that, Steve had been determined to make her miserable. First, he tried to spread rumors with the men that she was pregnant by an English man. When that didn't work, he'd tried to ruin her father's reputation.

When Emma's father had learned what Steve had done, he politely asked him to leave. Steve had called him and old man, and had spat on his face, but had ultimately left their small Amish town, with hopes of finding an Amish wife in a nearby settlement to the South.

Unfortunately, with Steve gone the farm work had piled up.

Emma had gone out into the fields with her dad, trying to help with the harvest every day, but she was slow and had little understanding of how to run the equipment. Her father's old body looked so feeble and frail, as he struggled to heft bales of hay. Eventually, he'd slipped off the back of an old gray wagon and had cut his leg on the way down.

The leg was slow to heal, and even though Emma had applied endless salves and home remedies, nothing would make the wound close. "Oh, I'm fine," her father had said. Yet, Emma could tell that he was far from alright.

Then, two days ago, her father had pressed his fist to his chest, clutching his heart while he shook, red-faced and flustered with pain. Seemingly in slow motion, he'd slumped over into the living room chair with a low howl as she rushed to his side. "Papa!" Emma had screamed, yet he'd only stared off into the distance as thick pools of saliva collecting in the corners of his mouth. Her father was gasping for air, frozen in pain, as Emma patted his back and tried to get him to answer her as his eyes darted from side to side.

As if that wasn't enough, Emma knew the situation was serious when her dear father had begun to converse with what seemed to be the ghost of his long-dead wife. His sunken eyes glared off into nothingness as he muttered, "Oh Anne, you look so lovely, darling. I love you so much. Hold my hand, beautiful girl. Promise you'll never leave my side." He spoke to his dead wife and to no one else, no matter how hard Emma and the others tried to get his attention.

After that, a rumor had started to swirl that that he'd been taken by an evil spirit. People had begun to talk—to say that her father had been a selfish man, which hadn't been true. There were countless times that he'd lent money to neighbors and had given away his crops for free. Yet, the Amish were often superstitious people and when so much tragedy struck a single household they sometimes blamed the members of the family.

Emma needed the Bishop to both dispel that rumor and to approve her father's treatment at a nearby English hospital. Many Amish within their community had come to visit, bearing all kinds of natural remedies, bringing baked goods, pungent salves, and endless prayers, yet nothing improved his condition.

Panicked, on the day he'd collapsed, Emma had dashed from their small farmhouse over into her neighbor's wide yard, screaming for help. The entire Johnson family had rushed over, at first fearing a farming accident. Later, the young women had kept watch with her every evening since then.

They slept dutifully in shifts, hovering over dad—turning him to avoid bed sores, spooning small amounts of water into his mouth, changing his soiled linens, and swapping out the bandage on his injured leg, which seemed to grow worse with each passing day. All the while, her father never even acknowledged their presence. He simply muttered to his darling deceased wife and stared off into the distance. However, most of the time he slept.

"What do you suppose is keeping the Bishop so long?" Emma asked her friend Ruth. Ruth shook her head. "I heard a rumor that he was all the way in Lancaster County visiting a dying widow when your papa fell sick. My cousin said that when our good Bishop got word of your father's illness he made haste in this direction, but it's a long journey by horse-drawn carriage, Emma. Plus, the weather hasn't been very good. I'm sure he's well on his way though, dear friend. Try not to worry; he'll know what to do."

Yet, all Emma could do was worry. There was so much at stake.

Emma sat down, tucking her hands into her apron. The wind tousled her blonde hair as she sighed deeply. "On days like today I wish I'd just joined the English and left this horrible place behind."

Ruth shot her friend an icy look, which then softened as she rubbed her friend's back, understanding that the stress of recent events was finally taking its toll on her. "I suppose it's the hardest to follow this path when things are difficult, but Heavenly Father promises us rewards beyond measure, Emma. Don't let the stress of the situation take you down with it. Everything will be okay."

Emma nodded her thanks blankly. She'd be able to calm down after her dad had seen a doctor, after the English had managed to restore him to his vibrant boisterous self, but not a moment before. The Bishop was taking far too long, and every moment that passed, things only grew worse.

When she'd been on her Rumspringa, years ago, there had a been a situation involving one of her teenage friends, which had resulted in a trip to an English hospital. The young man's name had been Noah Brown and he'd collapsed during a dance party, where he lay convulsing on the floor. "Are you okay, man?" A boy had asked, gently kicking him with a shoe.

They'd crowded around their dear friend, weak drinks in hand, not knowing what to do. Not having any adult leadership in the strange new English world, they had no way of knowing when a situation called for medical attention. It was Emma who had quickly declared that Noah needed help.

Finally, someone had run outside and asked for help. An older woman who'd been randomly passing by with her dog, used her cellphone to dial 9-1-1 and the paramedics had arrived within a matter of short minutes.

Emma had accompanied Noah to the hospital, mostly because no one else had wanted to. He'd grasped her hand while he was lying in the back on the stretcher. In that moment, for some reason he'd reminded her of her brother and her heart had opened to him. In their Amish world, she was used to seeing men in power and men in charge, but Noah was different. Even though he was strong, he also allowed himself to feel things and to be vulnerable—she admired that about him.

Two days later, after all the tests had been run on Noah, Emma had been the only one by his side when the English doctor had quietly come in and regrettably announced that Noah had a rare form of blood cancer. She'd never be able to forget the look in Noah's eyes then, as he reached for her—a complete stranger to hold him. She'd wrapped him in her arms and had held him as if they'd been friends for years instead of just a few days. "Can you stay?" He asked her. Emma had nodded silently.

So, while the rest of their friends spent their Rumspringa in clubs partying and swallowing down liquor, she'd spent hers gently holding

Noah's hand during his blood tests and endless other procedures. She'd gotten to know the hospital staff, but more importantly, she'd gotten to know Noah.

Somehow hours turned into days and before she knew it, she'd spent her entire Rumspringa by his side. Noah had actually wanted to return to the Amish, so that he could join the church and be with his family. Yet, the chemotherapy treatments he needed to live were forbidden by their community. Noah knew that if he left the English world, he would surely die. He could not go back to the Amish as they had no advanced medicine.

A week before Emma was due to return to the Amish, Noah had reached out for her. "Stay with me," he'd said softly. While most people had spent their Rumspringa in a haze of partying and drinking, virtually their entire time had been spent inside the English hospital.

They'd so often curled up in his bed together and flipped through the many television channels and free magazines that the nurses provided. In between treatments, she'd sometimes push his wheelchair down into the lobby where they'd listen to a nightly pianist, wordlessly holding hands. Then, they'd head back upstairs where they'd pick a movie from the hospital's offerings, and usually fall asleep arm in arm.

They weren't supposed to sleep like that—with her curled up in his hospital bed, but usually the nurses looked the other way and pretended not to notice. After all, he was dying.

In just a few short weeks Noah had become a part of her, and even now she sometimes woke up in the dead of night, hoping to find his scraggly blonde head of curls lying beside her. Even though that was years ago, she never could quite get over Noah. Emma had secretly thought that she'd probably miss him every day for the rest of her life, and she was okay with that. Noah was amazing.

In fact, the first time that Steve had asked her to be his girlfriend and to officially start courting, she'd said no because Steve was so different from Noah. For an Amish person, Steve had some serious character deficits. Plus, they never laughed together for hours on end the way she'd done with Noah.

Emma and Noah seemed to have just fit together seamlessly, and with Steve everything felt forced and unnatural. Noah was her first love and he wouldn't be easily forgotten. Often, Emma would lay awake in her bed, wondering if he'd made it through chemotherapy, just hoping he was somehow still alive. Maybe they'd meet again in heaven. Maybe one day she'd be lucky enough to just pass him on the street—to just catch one more glimpse of him.

Chapter 2

It was Emma who had pushed Noah to stay in the strange new English world, even though she knew it meant that she'd never see him again. Yet, at least it meant he'd be alive. "I want to be where you are," Noah had said, trying to stand. He reached for her and Emma shook her head no.

"You know that we don't have powerful medicine in our community. They'll cover you in herbs and they'll pray over you, but you'll die, Noah. And you and I both know it won't be a peaceful death." She said. He'd nodded in silent understanding. "Use the English medicine to get well, find a wife for yourself. Live and be happy. Give yourself a chance." Emma said, with tears in her eyes. "What if I don't know how to be happy without you? What if I don't want a life that doesn't have you in it?" Noah said, his voice shaking.

"And what if this isn't the way things are supposed to be?" He asked. "What do you mean?" Emma had questioned him. "What if the Lord brought us together because He meant for you to be my wife all along? What if we're meant to be together?" Noah kissed the back of her hand with his soft lips. She kissed him on the forehead and then turned away. "I'm sure the Lord wants you to be alive more than he wants anything else for you, Noah," she'd said. "What if I want to be with you more than I care about anything else?" Noah asked.

Then, she gave him one last hug. They stood locked together for a long time. Noah squeezed his eyelids shut, trying to remember the feel of her, her smile, every single detail of what it was like to hold Emma in his arms, just in case he never saw her again. Her body felt so perfect in his arms. Just touching her, made him feel a deep kind of peace.

"I'll never forget you, Noah," she said as she squeezed him tight, before exiting the room. The moment she was out of sight, she could hear that Noah had started to cry...but she couldn't turn back. She had to go back to the Amish, and if he tried to follow her, he would pay the price with his life.

In this one instance, true love meant walking away. Walking away from Noah was the hardest thing she'd ever done.

When Emma had returned to her father in their small Amish community, she'd put all her efforts into life on the farm, trying to push the memory of Noah's gentle touch out of her mind. Oh, how she hoped he was still alive. Maybe, he'd somehow found a wife and was married with children by now. Hopefully, he was happy—wherever he was.

Emma looked in the direction of her father's bedroom. Besides, her dad needed her. Even if she left the Amish and tried to find him, how would she even get started? Where would she look? There were millions of people on the planet. It was unlikely she'd ever be able to find him again.

Now that her father was ill, Emma had no idea of how to run the family farm. She knew how to bake and keep the house in good condition, but had no knowledge of farming or carpentry—and so many of their small structures had fallen into a state of disrepair. It was too bad that her brother Joshua had left them too. During his Rumspringa, he'd met a girl named Lily, and had announced to both she and their father that he would not be returning to Amish life.

It had been a slow descent downhill since then.

First, their cow Bessie died. They'd found her, laying belly-up in the pasture with white foam oozing out of her nose and mouth. Then, around three-quarters of their crops had been eaten by locusts. Emma secretly wondered if the plague might come next. But why? She and her father were dutiful and hard-working. Neither of them were arrogant or cruel. Had something angered the Maker of the universe? She had no way of knowing.

Emma sat on the sofa in the front room and slowly drifted to sleep. All the events of the past few days had weighed so heavily on her. Even though her neighbors had offered tremendous love and support, she couldn't rest. She'd lay in bed and toss and turn, feeling strange about the fact that her best friend was tending to her father while she was lying in bed. Something about that felt wrong to her.

Plus, Emma worried that it could give people the wrong impression. What kind of daughter rests when her father is dying? Yet, his illness had dragged on for days, and now sleep took hold, even though she'd fought it at every turn.

Emma drifted into a heavy sleep and felt a vague awareness that someone had placed a blanket over her. She gave a weak smile out of thanks.

In her dream, she found herself standing in the middle of their small church. There was an older gentleman standing before her, knitting a sweater—which was a strange sight for her. None of the men in her community knew how to knit. "Do you need help with that?" Emma asked.

The old man looked up from his knitting and smiled at her. "Oh, I'm fine. You know, all things always work together for good." He said, quoting scripture. Emma sat down beside him. "What else can you teach me?" She asked. "Oh, I'm not your teacher," the man chuckled. "Love is your teacher."

Love is your teacher.

Chapter 3

Emma woke to someone gently shaking her shoulders. It was her best friend Ruth. The Bishop had finally arrived.

Emma peeled the blanket off, as she stood and nodded towards him. "Where is your father?" the Bishop asked, as he clutched a hat to his chest. He was wet with rainwater and was dripping small puddles onto the wood flooring.

"He's in the back bedroom," Emma answered—leading the way. The Bishop's boots clopped heavily as he made his way across the living room. He stood by her father's bedside and clasped his hand tightly to her father's fist. Then the Bishop turned to her, "your father is surely dying." He said, flatly. Emma nodded, while tears welled in her eyes. Even though she'd suspected it for some time, it was painful to hear someone else say the words out loud. It brought a strange sort of finality to her father's illness.

"If you see fit, will you please allow me to take him to the hospital though? During my Rumspringa I learned that the English world has some powerful medicine and I'd like to take him there." The Bishop's eyes looked thoughtfully down at her father's face. Then, finally he nodded. "If it will bring you peace, do as you wish." Then, the Bishop knelt softly at her father's bed and said a few prayers. Then, he quietly exited their small home, and continued on his way to visit the next family in need of his help.

"Hurry Ruthie!" Emma called. Her friend rushed into the room and they worked hard to sit her father up. No matter how they positioned him, he slumped over like a sack of potatoes, unable to hold himself up. Finally, the boys jumped in and simply lifted him out to the horse drawn carriage. Emma breathed a sigh of relief as the horses pulled him all towards the nearby emergency room. Maybe the English could help. They were her last chance.

When they arrived, Emma was shocked at the level of haste with which the orderlies responded. They placed her father on a stretcher with tremendous ease, shouting orders among themselves and rushed him off. "Go with him!" Ruth called to her from inside the coach. Emma looked back for a brief second. "Thank you, Ruth. May the good Lord keep you!" She called.

The inside of the hospital was a lot noisier than she remembered. Doctors and nurses rushed around her father and began hooking him up to an IV. "Sir? Can you hear me, sir?" A doctor asked while shining a light into her father's pupils. "How long has he been like this?" The doctor asked her. Emma wasn't sure of how to answer. The doctor clarified. "How long has your father been unresponsive?" The doctor rephrased, a little more forcefully. "Nine days," Emma answered.

The doctor's rage was almost palpable. "So, you left him in this condition for nine days before it occurred to you that he might need serious help?" He asked. Emma shook her head. "I had to wait for the Bishop, or else he'd have been excommunicated. That would break my father's heart so it wasn't an option," she said softly. "I see," the doctor said. His tone was cold.

"And I don't imagine your father's ever actually been to a real doctor. Am I correct?" Tears welled up in Emma's eyes. She'd expected that the English would help her father, not blame her for abiding by the laws within her community. She'd done things exactly as her father would have wanted.

Emma stood back, watching as they hooked her dad up to an IV on one arm and started taking blood out from the other. She felt certain that the procedure had to hurt, but her father didn't even wince. The doctor yelled more orders to people and individuals in lab coats rushed in and out of the room. A catheter was placed into her dad, and he was dressed in a diaper. She watched as her father—her strong hero, lay there like some kind of comatose infant.

A few minutes later, a nurse rushed in and handed the doctor a few papers. The doctor looked over at Emma. "He's in a coma because he has sepsis. That infection on his leg made its way to his bloodstream, and then I'd guess that the stress of that caused him to have a heart attack. If you'd have brought him to me nine days ago, I could have fixed this, but you waited so long. I have no idea if we'll be able to save him."

Her father let out a grunt, as if he'd heard the doctor's words, and then suddenly flatlined. The entire room sprung into chaos in mere seconds.

They pressed electric paddles to his heart over and over again, while epinephrine was pushed into his IV. Finally, her father's heart was beating again—yet he looked even worse than before. Now, he was intubated and he looked like some kind of corpse on a breathing machine.

"This is a very hard lesson for you." The doctor said as he exited the room. Emma reached over and squeezed her father's hand. Perhaps the doctor was right. Perhaps she should have just taken him to the hospital without waiting on the Bishop's permission. Maybe her obedience had been foolish.

Just then, a machine made a loud beeping sound again. Doctors flooded into the room for a second time. Again, they used the paddles, trying to restart his heart over and over. "Papa?" Emma whispered, when it was clear to her that all their efforts to save his life weren't working this time. "Get her out of here!" The doctor yelled. "Papa!" Emma screamed.

He was gone.

Chapter 4

Emma walked out of the hospital room in a mental fog. Everything had happened so quickly that it felt like a dream. Even worse, all the responsibility was on her shoulders now. There was no one to run the farm but her. No one to plan the funeral, but her. She would have to carry on somehow, but all of a sudden, for the first time in her life she felt totally alone. The weight of all that responsibility felt as though it could crush her.

Emma found her way out of the hospital's double doors and sat down on a bench. It was raining lightly outside, but she didn't care. She pulled off her bonnet and threw it into the street, not really knowing why and watched as a speeding car flattened it into the pavement.

Then, she began to sob into her hands, without any regard for who might be around. Her father—the man that had raised her, protected her, and provided for her, was now gone forever. She was the only one left.

Someone placed a soft hand on her shoulder. "Emma?" The voice asked. "Emma, is that you?"

Emma turned slowly, letting her eyes adjust to the light. She recognized him at once when she saw the curly mop of yellow hair and the kind eyes. "Noah?" She asked. "Yes," he answered. At once, she threw her arms around him and sobbed into his shirt for what seemed like hours. When they finally peeled their bodies apart she was so overwhelmed she thought she might faint.

She wanted to say that she'd prayed for this moment, that she'd thought of him every day for years, always wondering if he was still alive, but the words wouldn't come out of her lips. Noah stroked her hair gently. "We need to get you inside and out of this rain," Noah finally said. Even through her grief she could tell that he was healthy now. His once frail body was now muscular and tan. He even seemed taller than she remembered and he walked around easily, guiding her by the hand.

Noah led her down a long corridor into the hospital café, where he ordered her a small cup of hot chocolate. Then, he gently led her by the hand and they sat together in a booth in the back. "I'm so sorry about your father," Noah finally said.

Emma nodded, still having difficulty processing the situation. "Why are you here?" She asked after a long while. "I was visiting a friend. I did exactly what you told me to do. I stayed here and went to the cancer ward. I married one of the girls I met there." His eyes were sad when he said that part.

"What a lucky woman she is, "Emma said with a weak smile. "Was" Noah corrected her. "She died a year ago from brain cancer." He said.

"I'm sorry," Emma said. Noah shook his head. "There's no need for you to be sorry. You saved my life." He smiled at her and then reached forward to push a few fingers through her long hair. "I just got a clean bill of health this month," Noah said. "Your Amish Bishop won't take me back, but a more liberal Amish group said that I can come back. I was going to look for you as soon as I did." He said.

Somehow Noah's presence made her heart feel lighter. Even with the heaviness of just losing her father, she felt safe and protected near him. "I'm buying the Johnson's farm." Noah added.

Chapter 5

Two months later, Emma hugged Ruth goodbye as the entire Johnson family packed into their horse-drawn carriage. Noah had made good on his plans, and had bought their family farm for a fair price.

Now, they were headed south with plans of opening a cheese farm. He had joined a nearby Amish church, though one slightly more liberal than Emma's parish. Noah's new church had both understood and respected Noah's choice to seek cancer treatment, and they'd welcomed him with open arms.

With Ruth and her family gone, things were incredibly quiet on the farm. Emma had managed to set a routine for herself, rising just as the sun was starting to peak through the morning sky and toiling until dark.

A few boys from the church had come on as hired hands, and with their help, she'd managed to stay afloat. Often, when he wasn't working his own land, Noah would come over to help her out. They'd heft barrels of hay and then spend long hours on the front porch drinking lemonade, chatting about the future. It was a lot like the old days. Except of course, for the Bishop.

Ever since her father had died, the Bishop had been giving Emma a hard time. In keeping with their traditions, he felt that Emma should sign her farm over to him, yet she refused to do so. What if the Bishop then decided to kick her off her land? She'd have nowhere to go. Plus, she'd worked so hard throughout the years. The farmhouse was her home.

One day, when Emma was working in the fields with the boys and Noah, a figure appeared in the distance. He was lean and wiry and walked with a limp. Emma strode out to see who it was, with a strange feeling in the pit of her stomach. Low and behold, it was her ex-boyfriend Steve. He was holding a heavy duffel bag and looked somewhat defeated.

"Emma!" Steve called when he saw her. Her voice got caught in her throat. He looked ragged and had those same mean eyes that she never felt could be trusted.

"It's been a long time, Steve," Emma finally said politely. "I missed you so much. I went to that Amish community I told you about, but they kicked me out. I heard about your father's death and I figured you might need a hand, so I packed up and came to help." Emma looked suspiciously at his bag. She didn't want him to stay. He'd scarcely been there for five minutes, and Emma already wanted him to go.

"You got anything to eat?" Steve asked. Emma looked over at the boys and Noah. "We have a lot of work that we have to finish by sundown, but if you want, I'll fix you something to eat after that." Emma said pointedly. "You're working in the fields now?" Steve asked. "We do what we must...and anyway, I enjoy it. It's a good work-out." Emma said, skipping back over to where the men were still lifting bails.

Steve threw down his duffle bag and angrily went to join in. Emma watched as Steve and Noah's eyes met. She could tell from Noah's expression that he didn't like Steve and that Steve didn't like him either.

She made quick introductions and then they continued to work in silence until the sun set. All their laughter had ended when Steve had arrived.

Later, that evening, Emma fixed dinner for Noah, Steve, and the two boys she'd hired. It was a hearty meal of fried chicken, mashed potatoes, green beans, and yeast rolls. As she set a plate in front of Noah, he winked at her and smiled. Steve caught the moment that was shared between them and scoffed.

"So tell me, Noah, how long have you known my girlfriend?" Steve asked, after everyone had started to eat. Noah looked up, confused. "You never told me you were dating anyone?" He said. "That's because I'm not dating anyone." Emma answered, without skipping a beat. "Steve broke up with me a long time ago. I haven't seen him in months." The boys chuckled and everyone at the table nodded. Steve's face was beet red.

"Well, since your father's passing I knew you'd need a hand in running the farm." Steve said snidely.

"I don't know, it seems to me like Emma's doing a mighty fine job," Noah said, smiling at her from across the table. Noah looked over at Steve's bag which was now resting on the floor.

"I can use my horse to take you to one of the Inns downtown," Noah said to Steve. "Surely you weren't expecting to stay here alone with Emma, since you aren't married—as I'm sure you realize that could endanger her reputation with the church." Steve looked so furious Emma feared he might explode.

"And since when did you become the authority on the church?" Steve asked. "You belong to that liberal Amish group, don't you?" Steve asked. Everyone at the table grew quiet. "You call hem liberal. I call them sensible," Noah said after a long while.

When dinner was over, Noah made sure that Steve left with him. He drove him downtown in his carriage and helped him with the expense of a hotel, for which Steve did not even say thank you.

As Emma cleaned up, she couldn't help but smile to herself. Only a few months ago, she'd thought she would never see Noah again and now here he was, living right next door to her, protecting her.

Chapter 6

The next morning, the Bishop showed up on her doorstep, with a loud knock. He held a document in his hand and shoved it at Emma as he pushed his way into her house. "Last night, Steve came to me and told me that you're living in sin," the Bishop snarled. "Is it true that you've had men in this home without chaperones?" The Bishop demanded. Emma swallowed.

"I have two young Amish boys that work the land for me, and sometimes my neighbor Noah is kind enough to come over and help me with the farm." The Bishop looked her up and down with a scowl.

"You are a disgrace," he finally said. "You know that it is against the rules of our church for you to be alone with strange men. We don't allow that. Lucky for you though, Steve Ingalls has agreed to marry you and save your ruined reputation."

Just then, Steve let himself into her home. Emma's eyes widened. "Steve is a member of our church in good standing and will make a suitable match for you. Otherwise, if you choose not to marry, I'm going to call an inquest and have this farm taken from you. Those are your options."

The Bishop turned and snidely let himself out of the home, just as Emma collapsed into tears.

Through her crying, she could hear Steve chuckling. "You always thought you were so much better than me, didn't you?" Steve said. "Well, look who gets to have the last laugh now?" Steve stood and grabbed her hard by the wrist. Then, he pressed her against the wall and pushed her dress to the side. Emma screamed.

Before Steve could say another word, Noah had burst through the door and had thrown Steve onto the floor.

"Don't you ever lay a hand on her!" He yelled. Steve's mouth was bloody and he looked up at them with hateful eyes. "Get out of my house and don't ever come back." Emma said softly.

Steve brushed himself off and stood up. Then, he stopped dead in his tracks. He turned around and smiled. "Emma,I'm sorry that I never got to poison you, like I did your old cow Bessie. I'd have gotten rich, if I could have gotten you out of the way."

Steve shot Emma a nasty look and Noah stepped in front of her. "You'd have to get through me first, Steve and by the looks of it, I don't think that's ever gonna happen."

Emma clasped Noah's hand in her own as she watched Steve walk down the long dirt road and drift out of sight, out of her life forever.

As soon as Steve was out of sight, again Emma collapsed into tears. She told Noah the entire story in a rush. She had to either get married or lose the farm. "Well, that's great news!" Noah smiled. Emma looked at him for a moment as though he'd gone mad. "Well, now I finally have an excuse to make you my wife." He said, leaning in and kissing her deeply.

Chapter 7

Two weeks later, Emma was smiling from ear to ear as she walked down the aisle towards Noah. After the Bishop's threats, she'd made the decision to join Noah's Amish parish and they had welcomed her with open arms. She'd never felt more beautiful as she made her way through the wooden chapel, to stand beside Noah. Her first love; her only love.

After the ceremony, they danced the night away. With banjos and fiddles in full-swing, and all the delicious food of the Amish, Emma had never felt so happy in all her life.

Later that evening, after most of the guests had departed an older Amish man slowly made his way forward and presented the new couple with a wrapped gift. When Emma pulled the wrapping off, she was surprised to find a knitted heart.

"I'm so glad to know that you both found your way home. Isn't love a wonderful teacher?" the old man muttered as he shuffled away. Emma looked at Noah with tears in her eyes as she leaned back and laughed. Love had shown them both the way.

AMISH CREEK

MONICA MARKS

Winter

The night had taken on a cold chill and it was somehow fitting of the heaviness in Jacob's heart. He gently urged the horses forward as they shied from an oncoming car, carefully guiding them closer to the ditch at the side of the road. Ahead of his carriage were two more, one for each of his brothers and their respective wives. The family was approaching the market and Jacob was grateful for his hands were slowly freezing against the reins despite the heavy woolen gloves covering them. The three carts eased into the wide parking area to the left of the treeline and Eliza, Jacob's younger sister-in-law, was the first out of carriage, already busying herself with the merchandise in the back of the wagon. By the time Jacob pulled his horses to a full stop, she had managed to unload a substantial number of goods. She smiled briefly at him as he approached to assist her but waved him away.

"It's all right, Jacob, I am quite capable of handling this here. You can go about whatever you need to do in your carriage." Jacob nodded but said nothing. He had never been one to say much.

"That's why you're not married," Jonah would tease him. "The women have no idea what you're thinking. How are they supposed to know that you have marriage on your mind when you say so little?" Jonah had no way of knowing how his words upset Jacob as it was merely meant to be brotherly teasing but Jacob often wished that he was more outspoken. Yet when he was in the presence of his female peers, he found himself more tongue-tied than usual. Gabriel and Jonah often pointed out the blue painted gates of the eligible women in town but Jacob always averted his eyes and changed the subject or maintained complete silence. Eliza and Jonah had just wed the previous month and as his just barely younger brother hopped down to join his new wife, Jacob could not help but feel a pang of envy at the new scruff covering his sibling's face. Subconsciously, Jacob found himself touching his own clean shaven, soft cheek, wondering if he would ever be able to boast the beard of a married man.

"Come along now, Jacob," Gabriel urged suddenly appearing at his side. "The cheese will freeze if you stand here too long."

"Really, Jacob," Louisa scowled. "You know better than to stand there while our goods go bad." At the sound of his older sister-in-law's voice, Jacob shifted his eyes downward and picked up the pace of unpacking the freshly churned cheese onto the wheelbarrows Eliza had dug out from the depth of her cart. Louisa was the dark, complete opposite of Jonah's sweet natured, cheerful mate. Louisa was only a year older than Jacob but she looked and acted like Jacob's ninety-year-old grandmother. She was starch and rigid and unlike Jacob's beloved grandmother, never had a kind word to say. Jacob could never understand why his older brother, Gabriel had married such an embittered woman. Gabriel was without a doubt the most attractive and hardest working member of their family. He was mild mannered and intelligent and he could have had his pick of any number of eligible women in their community. However, that was neither here nor there at that moment as Louisa's look of anger was deepening by the second as she watched Jacob's idling. Gabriel took the wheelbarrow from Jacob's hands, also noticing the look on Louisa's face and followed Jonah and Eliza toward the indoor market, Jacob close behind them, Louisa on his heels like a rabid sheepdog trying to keep in in line. Once inside, Jacob was relieved for the wood burning stoves which were filled with fresh wood and already warming the giant barn, despite the early morning hour. Someone had taken care to ensure the vendors were comfortable upon their arrival. It was barely six o'clock and the winter sun had yet to break through the blackness of night but the smell of the wood against cold winter air brought a surge of familiar melancholy to Jacob. He had been feeling lost the past few months, as if he were missing a key element, like air or water. He suspected that Jonah's wedding had helped bring about the sudden loneliness. *You need to find a wife and start a family. You're twenty-five years old. You are the last man in the family and you're unmarried. Even your younger brother is married before you! That is shameful!* Louisa's sharp tone snapped him out of his brooding.

"Are you going to stand there until the sun goes down, Jacob?" He shuffled forward without looking up, joining the rest of his family at their booth. He liked this venue. It was a true Amish market, lit with soft gaslights and no electricity. It had once been an old, neglected barn belonging to a vast colonial house but years after the family who had owned it went bankrupt, the land was distributed among the Amish communities evenly. The house had been demolished and Jacob's family lived on one part of the fruitful farmland, raising goats, cows and chickens. They had been dairy farmers for generations. A neighboring district had reconstructed the dilapidated barn, expanding it to four times its size and they had created a small trader's market within the grand structure. Everyone was welcome, provided they respected the land. On any given day from Tuesday to Saturday, there were merchants selling jams and quilts, sweaters and meats. Only the freshest vegetables and cheeses could be found in the simple wooden booths, packed in ice and metal buckets. Once in a while, a more ambitious traveler would set up a crate boasting homemade wine or cider but those peddlers were becoming more and more scarce as the demand for their supply diminished. While it was open to the general public, it maintained the virtue in which Jacob was raised and he felt more at home at this particular location than any of the others at which they frequented over the year. Their cheeses were on display in a very short time and now there was little else to do but wait for traffic. Eliza immediately sat upon a skid of wood and began knitting while Louisa seemed content to stand back, arms folded and tight lipped, sternly watching the vendors prepare to the upcoming day.

"Did you bring something to read, Jacob?" Eliza asked brightly, smiling at him. Jacob nodded quickly and lowered his blue eyes, blushing. Her smile widened but she did not tease him. Jonah, however, seized the opportunity.

"We are ever so grateful that you did, Jacob! Otherwise you might never stop talking!" Jacob reached into his burlap sack to remove a book he had recently borrowed from the library in Lancaster, ignoring his brother.

"Leave him alone," Gabriel growled at Jonah. "At least he knows when to stay quiet."

"Oh, quiet yourself, Gabriel. If I can't tease Jacob, who can?"

"No one needs to bother Jacob," Eliza piped in pleasantly. "I think it's wonderful that he has such a disposition. It will take him far in life."

Jacob almost hugged his new sister. Instead he offered her a timid smile before looking back down at the pages before him.

"No one needs to be silent all the time," Louisa retorted. "Really, Jacob, how are you going to court anyone without learning how to speak?"

"That's enough!" Gabriel snapped. Everyone looked at him in surprise, including Jacob. "Jacob will marry when the time is right and he will speak to someone when he finds someone worthy of hearing his voice. Now leave him be!" Inexplicably, tears sprung into Jacob's eyes. Jonah looked abashed while Louisa looked contrite.

"Of course," Louisa mumbled, retreating to her spot against a post. Gabriel drew close to his younger brother.

"There is nothing wrong with you. You are patient, kind and you will make a just minister to our district one day. Don't let anyone tell you otherwise."

"Thank you, brother," Jacob murmured. Gabriel patted him reassuringly on the shoulder and went to join his wife. Jacob watched him walk away and wondered if that speech of confidence was actually for him or if Gabriel was just thinking to himself aloud.

The day got colder even as the sun fought to break through the ominous clouds. A storm was brewing and the market was suffering as a result. Only a few people had dared venture out as the temperatures dropped to a desolate, inconsolable place. It was the kind of day where even the marrow of the bones was chilled and could not be warmed under any circumstance. Most of the patrons were tourists passing through Amish country but a few neighboring communities stopped by to provide their support. Jacob was happy he had thought to bring along another book as he had barely had occasion to raise his eyes from the first one he had packed. Then fate mysteriously intervened.

It started as a shriek. Startled, Jacob looked up and blinked as an object came hurling at his head. Out of nowhere, a body slammed into his and he was belly down under the neighboring booth, Gabriel on top of him. A peal of child's laughter rang out, followed by a group chuckle and it was clear that whatever had occurred had merely been the act of a clumsy or mischievous child. But as Jacob rose put his hands down to raise his body up, his eyes locked upon a pair of light brown irises, crouched down like a preying tiger directly at his level. There was a face inches from his underneath the table, their lips almost touching one another. And suddenly Jacob was not in the din of the market any longer.

They skipped in a circle, the long grasses tickling their knees as the group picked up speed. The scent of wildflowers and herbs filled the air. Jacob's head was feeling light and he wasn't sure if it were as a result of the dizzying game or the beautiful eyes of his classmate, Grace which seemed to be fixated on his own. Even at the tender age of eight, Jacob recognized the impossible beauty of those orbs, a luminous, liquid brown, so light they seemed gold in the springtime sunlight. The round dance continued a few more laps until Grace herself "tripped" and landed the group into an unceremonious pile of young, panting bodies onto the lea. Yet through the reeds, Grace still stared at him and he at her. And not once did he feel the urge to look away in shyness.

"Jacob!" the eyes spoke. Quickly, Jacob lifted his head to stand and hit his skull against the booth, creating a sickening crack at the impact. His hand raised instinctively to his head.

"Oh! Are you all right?" She was at his side, grabbing his arm in aide. Jacob was immediately torn. He knew that he was not supposed to have this kind of contact with an outsider but this outsider was different...she was Grace.

"Uh...yes, thank you. Hello Grace," he mumbled, staring up at her. "How are you?"

Grace smiled that off-centered, charming grin which could disarm the angriest of bees.

"I'm well, Jacob. I'm so happy to see you here! I have been here a few times in the last months but you are never here when I come. I have been yearning for your goat cheese for years now and I finally had the courage to come around. Have you any for sale? Truly you can't find anything like your family's cheeses in the city."

Jacob nodded and before he could lead her around to the booth, he was looking up directly into Louisa's scowling face.

"Come along, Jacob," Louisa intervened, pulling him from Grace. "You're needed."

"But she wants – "Jacob protested.

"Eliza can help her," Louisa snapped. "Eliza! Help this woman!"

Louisa almost spat the word "woman" as she scathingly glared at Grace. Grace looked forlorn as she watched his sister-in-law shuffle him away. She slowly raised a gloved hand and smiled sadly as he looked back at her.

"Bye Jacob," she mouthed.

"You should know better, Jacob," Gabriel chided. They were back in their home, gathered by the warm hearth of the fire, counting their profits from the day. Jonah and Eliza looked up questioningly.

"Oh do tell! What could our patient Jacob possibly have done to earn trouble?" Eliza joked. "This I must hear!"

"Your brother-in-law was fraternizing with a fallen woman, a shunned member of this community," Louisa snapped. "Looking after her like some lost lamb. You should be ashamed of yourself, Jacob! You are just asking for trouble!"

"Who?" Eliza and Jonah chorused. "Which shunned woman?"

"That Beiler woman," Gabriel replied quietly. Eliza's eyes lit up.

"Lydia?" she squealed. "Oh how is she?"

Louisa's frown deepened into her characteristic scowl.

"No, the other one. Grace. Their poor, shamed parents. Can you imagine? Having two of your children living scandalously in the city? What are the odds of that occurring? It's no surprise they're in such poor health."

"Jacob, you saw Grace today?" Naomi, Jonah's twin looked up from kneading bread to address her younger brother. "How did she look? Is she well?"

Jacob nodded. Naomi and Grace had been very close before Grace had left the church. Naomi had been devastated when Grace had been exiled and she had never completely recovered. Probably no more than Jacob had.

"She said she was well," Jacob replied.

"You spoke to her?" their father was incensed from his rocking chair at the hearth. "Jacob, I expect better from you!"

"She was there to buy cheese!" Gabriel jumped in. "You cannot make a sale if you do not speak with the customers, papa."

Jacob looked gratefully at his brother.

"In the future, you let the women handle the women," their father muttered. All the siblings exchanged a secret smile, except, of course, Louisa.

"Jacob, what a pleasant surprise. How are you?" The bishop looked up from a pile of papers and smiled at the man in his doorway. "Please come in."

"Hello, Bishop. Is this an opportune time?"

"Of course! I don't get to see enough of you. Oh! Wait! I know what this is about! You're here to announce a betrothal!" The heavy set man clapped his hands together, his eyes lighting up with happiness. "Who is the lucky woman?"

Jacob shook his head quickly and averted his expressive blue eyes.

"No, Bishop. It's not a marriage announcement..." The bishop read Jacob's somber expression and his smile faded. He gestured at a simple chair across from his desk.

"Please sit down," he encouraged the younger man. Jacob obliged, still staring at the floor.

"Is something wrong, Jacob?"

"No...well..." Jacob paused, unsure of how to word what he wanted to say. He wished he had asked Gabriel for advice before doing something this inane. If his father found out...well it was too late now.

"Bishop, if someone were to be excommunicated, could they ever come back?" Sighing, Bishop Fisher sat back against the rigid chair and pushed his spectacles off the bridge of his nose, onto his receding hairline.

"Jacob, the idea behind rumspringa is for you to see what waits for you beyond the security of our community. That is why we look the other way when the young people go and experiment with different aspects of the world in which we don't engage before making the very important choice of being baptized. Once you are baptized, we expect that you have 'sowed your wild oats' so to speak. So Jacob, if you are having a crisis of faith, we can help you through community and prayer but if you choose to leave the Amish community now, it will be very difficult for you to return. Realistically, I would say nearly impossible. "

Jacob laughed, startling the man.

"I'm sorry, Bishop. I didn't mean to laugh. You needn't worry about me. I have no desire to go anywhere away from my family and land. I was asking about someone else." The bishop looked slightly more relaxed but curiosity gleamed in his eye.

"Could you give me the circumstances?" he asked. Jacob suddenly realized his mistake. The community was too close. There was no possible way that this meeting would not reach the ears of his family. He was acting like a foolish child, making this trip and asking ridiculous questions. Why would he assume that Grace would ever want to come back? She most likely loved her life in the city. She and may even be married already! Shame stained his cheeks crimson and Jacob stood suddenly.

"I'm sorry, Bishop. This was a silly thing for me to do. I made a mistake." Without waiting for an answer, Jacob hurried out of the small house and down the road toward his farm.

Jacob was about to vomit. He could feel the bile raising to his mouth, creating a pool of saliva under his tongue. *Don't get ill! You foolish, foolish man! What are you doing here?*

An elderly woman smiled kindly at him and handed him a paper bag from beside her seat.

"Motion sickness, honey?" she asked. Tentatively, Jacob accepted the bag. Then, to his horror, he retched into it. Surprisingly, after he was finished, he felt much better. The aging woman nodded knowingly.

"There you go. My grandson gets carsick too. He's only ten but I carry bags just in case. I didn't think people got carsick at your age," she told him.

"I've never been on a bus before," Jacob admitted. Her grinned widened and she nodded understandingly, taking in his simple, homespun clothing.

"Well that would explain it then. Just take deep breaths and try to relax. We'll be in Philadelphia in less than an hour." Jacob nodded and tried to heed her advice but his stomach would not settle. He imagined that had more to do with what he was doing than the actual bus ride itself. This was completely out of character for him. In fact, he could hardly believe what he was doing. He didn't know what he was hoping to accomplish but he also knew that since the day he had seen Grace in the market, he had been unable to think of anything but her. Her heart-warming smile was in the fireplace, her dark honey eyes were in the rays of sunlight streaking through the pines. He heard her voice in the chirping birds and once he thought he even saw her standing behind their barn but of course it had only been his mind playing tricks. He could not get her out of his head. He had to know if she was happy, if she thought of him or at least if she missed her life and her family in the district. Of course what he was doing was forbidden and if he were caught, he would be punished. But that would be the least of his problems. He would never hear the end of it from Louisa. Yet none of that seemed to matter. He would not rest until he knew that Grace was happy in her life. Even if that meant she was content without him.

As the older woman had predicted, less than an hour later, the bus was pulling into the hectic station in Philadelphia. Jacob had never seen such chaos. During rumspringa, he and Jonah had gone into town twice. Jonah had put on outsider clothing, smoked a cigarette and drank beer. Jacob had almost been sick from all of the foreign smells and the bustle. While he had accompanied his brother, he never felt the need to experiment with anything he did not know. There had never been any doubt that Jacob would be baptized. Unlike his peers, he had never felt the need go outside of is upbringing to see how good was their life. He recognized the purity in their way, the unity they had with nature and with each other. He couldn't imagine a life without the structural peace in which he had been reared. Jacob had always felt blessed by his birthright and respected the culture immensely. It was for all of these reasons that his underarms were soaked in perspiration at that moment, despite the crisp winter air. He nodded good-bye to his bus mate and slowly walked off the vehicle, his head swimming from all of the activity. *Stay focussed on your task, Jacob. You will be home before anyone realizes you are gone.* Once off the bus, he reached into the pocket of his plain brown pants and withdrew a scrap of paper. Then looking about, he spotted a taxi cab stop on the outskirts of the bustling station. Without hesitation, he made his way into a car and muttered the address written on the piece he was holding. The cabbie raised his eyebrow slightly at the sight of his passenger but made no comment at Jacob's outdated clothing.

"Is this your first time in Philly?" the man asked pleasantly, somehow feeling the need to put his obviously uncomfortable fare at ease. Jacob nodded quickly but stared out the window. His head was beginning to ache from all of the sights and sounds whizzing by the window.

"There's a lot of history here," the driver offered but when Jacob did not reply, he gave up and continued the relatively short trip to his destination. Jacob paid the charge and nodded before climbing onto the sidewalk. As the car drove away, he found himself looking back at the paper and then up at the apartment which he faced. He was in the right spot according to the phone book he had consulted at the Lancaster Library. This was Grace's home. For a moment, he considered aborting the mission all together and running back to the safety of Lancaster County. *But then you'll never know,* he told himself. And that was all the convincing he needed. He started up the steps and was inside the tiny entranceway, looking for her name on the intercom system. A teen boy walked out of the lobby and held the door open so Jacob slipped inside, rather than searching for the code. The phone book had declared Grace's apartment to be 401. Jacob opted for the stairs rather than the elevator. He reached the fourth floor and knocked on the door boasting 401 in scarred gold numbers. After a moment, he heard footsteps and a woman sing out.

"Coming!" Jacob swallowed and tried to prepare himself for coming face to face with the only woman who he had been able to speak with his entire life. But when the door flew open, it was not Grace. In Jacob's intense disappointment, he almost walked away, not realizing that he was looking at Lydia, Grace's younger sister.

"Jacob Miller! I don't believe my eyes!" she hollered. "Grace! You won't believe who is at our door!"

Jacob turned back to the doorway he was already departing, his eyes filled with hope at the sound of Grace's name.

"Is Grace here?" he asked, his voice no higher than a whisper. Lydia nodded eagerly and ushered him into the tiny apartment. Seconds later, Grace appeared in the hallway, her lava-like eyes wide with surprise.

"It really is you, Jacob! What – how...oh don't tell me you've been excommunicated!" Grace cried, rushing forward to embrace him in a hug. Not wanting to move but willing himself to do so, he stepped out of her friendly gesture and shook his head, color blushing his face with embarrassment.

"No...I...I came to see you, Grace," he said. "Is there any way we can speak? Just for a few moments?"

Lydia looked shocked but quickly nodded and said she was on her way out. She picked up a set of keys from the kitchen table and smiled briefly before flying out the door. Before she closed the door, she turned to Jacob, her eyes shiny.

"I understand that your brother wed Eliza Lapp. Please, if you find it in your heart, can you tell Eliza I think of her often?" Lydia did not wait for an answer and Jacob realized it was because she was about to cry. The door to the apartment closed and Grace smiled welcomingly at Jacob.

"Please, come and sit down. Can I offer you anything? A tea?" Jacob shook his head and sat down on the edge of an old velvet sofa.

"I can't tell you how wonderful it is to see you! I haven't been able to stop thinking about you since I saw you last week. I have been trying to find covert ways to see you and Naomi since I left. This has been my only fruitful attempt thus far. How is your sister?

Jacob nodded.

"She is well. She heard that I had seen you and asked the same. I believe she misses you very much, Grace." She smiled sadly.

"I miss her also. And I miss you, Jacob. You were my very first love." Jacob was stunned to hear the words. He had hoped, maybe even suspected that Grace had thought of him lovingly but he had always been far too bashful to find out if she held the same types of feelings for him. He felt like a weight had been lifted off his chest, a barbell which had resided upon him since the horrible day that Grace had left his life.

"Why don't you come back?" he asked her seriously. "Do you want to come back?"

Grace sat heavily back against the rocking chair in which she sat.

"Very much, Jacob but it is not that simple. If Lydia wanted to return, she would have a much easier time of it. She was never baptized so in theory, she never really left the church. She's basically on an extended rumspringa. I, on the other hand, have been baptized and I turned my back on my vows to our community."

"Why did you leave?" Jacob pressed before he could stop himself. He wasn't sure he wanted to hear the answer. He had always feared that she had fallen in love with an outsider. Grace's face fell.

"When Lydia began her rumspringa, it was just about a year after you and I had been baptized. Justine and Joseph had just gotten married and it was only Lydia and I left in the house with our parents. The workload doubled and I was fine with that but Lydia had always been willful. She began to act out and refuse to do the work. My parents' health had begun to fail at that point.

Suddenly, Lydia was not coming home at night and I would go looking for her and find her in cars with boys, high off marijuana, wearing skimpy clothing. I was only grateful my mother never had to witness anything of the sort or she would surely be dead by now of a heart attack. Night after night, I would drag Lydia home, pour cold water on her head and sober her up but this wasn't just a phase. I knew she was going to leave." Grace paused and looked up at Jacob.

"She is my little sister, Jacob. She is lost and naïve and doesn't know the ways of the world. She needed someone to protect her. She had no one…"

Jacob felt a lump grow in his throat. Grace was such an incredible sister. Would he do the same thing for Jonah or Naomi? He was ashamed but he knew that he would not. It took courage to do what she did for Lydia.

"How is Lydia doing now?" Jacob asked. He feared the answer.

"She is wonderful! She went to college and got a degree as a paralegal. She met a very nice man, a lawyer and I do believe he is going to propose any day now." Grace smiled but Jacob read the pain in her eyes.

"Do you want to come home?" Jacob asked again. Grace nodded slightly but changed her affirmative into a shrug.

"That's really not relevant, Jacob. I won't be welcomed back. I have learned to accept that fact. I knew what I was doing and this is my penance for making such a choice."

"You must speak to Bishop Fisher, Grace!" Jacob told her. She shook her head.

"You must go back home, Jacob and forget about me. If anyone finds out you were here…" She rose and went to guide him to the door.

"I can't tell you how wonderful it is to see you, Jacob. If you somehow find a way, tell your sister I miss her dearly. But don't put yourself into any trouble doing so." Instinctively, she reached out and embraced Jacob. Before he could stop himself, he had wrapped his own arms around her and relished the feeling of her closeness for one blissful moment. It might be the last time he ever had the opportunity.

"Good-bye, Jacob," she whispered in his ear and slowly closed the door, leaving him staring at it, troubled and confused.

"Bishop, is this an inopportune time?"

"Jacob! You left so quickly the other day, I thought it was something I had said!" the jovial man rose quickly from behind the scarred desk and hurried to greet Jacob at the door. "Please come in!"

Jacob moved further into the small office and sat before the elder, choosing his words carefully.

"Have you come to further discuss what we started the other day?" Jacob nodded.

"Sir, do you recall the Beiler sisters? Grace and Lydia?" The man frowned deeply, apparently troubled by the mention of their names.

"Yes," he replied slowly. "Why do you ask?"

"Grace would like to come home," Jacob answered simply. The Bishop began to shake his head at once but for the first time in his life, Jacob felt a rod of steel fuse into his spine and he sat up straight in his chair. He would not take no for an answer. Not this time.

"I do not think that is in the realm of possibility, son," the kindly man said. "Now if Lydia wanted to rejoin us, that might be possible since she has yet to be baptized however, it would be a process – "

"Lydia is very happy living in the outside world. Grace knows her place is here with us." The bishop continued to shake his head and Jacob felt his jaw clench, a motion that was foreign and unsettling to both men. Bishop Fisher seemed to recognize his anger at once and tried to diffuse the situation with logic.

"Jacob, what you are asking is out of the question. Grace Beiler chose to leave after she already committed herself to us. She not only abandoned our community, she left her own family to contend with an awful burden from both a labor and personal standpoint. Surely you cannot ignore those facts!" Jacob stared defiantly at Bishop Fisher.

"You don't know all of the facts, Bishop or you would change your mind," Jacob almost spat between clenched teeth. "Grace Beiler is an honorable woman and she belongs here with her people. She is willing to repent and undergo whatever punishment you deem fit to allow her back but please, Bishop, you must consider this!" Again, the Bishop shook his head, his eyes misty with sadness.

"This is not my decision to make, Jacob. Grace already made the decision for herself. There is nothing I can do. You must forget about Grace Beiler. There are many eligible women who would be very fortunate to be wed to you, Jacob. Please try to focus on what is feasible. Grace Beiler is a dream." The Bishop stood up, indicating the conversation was done. Jacob felt familiar the lead weight of loneliness overwhelm his chest. He had known that this was apt to be the end result but he would have never forgiven himself if he had not given it a sincere chance. But he had failed. And Grace would never be there to untie his tongue as she had in childhood. As he slowly let himself outside into the cold winter afternoon, he somehow didn't see Grace's eyes in the sunlight for the first time since their encounter at the market.

Spring

The first day of warmth was a time for celebration among the Miller family. Although the temperatures had just barely climbed above freezing, it was enough to have melted the snow and cause a slushy mess for children to stomp around while the men bravely retired their heavy wool coats and the women dared leave the wash on the line all day without fear of freezing the handmade fabrics. Even Louisa seemed to be in a good mood as the brand new baby buds dripped snowflakes into puddles of water and caught the golden sunrays in their reflections. Louisa had just discovered she was with child and for the first time that anyone could remember, she was actually smiling. It was a lovely smile, in fact and quite infectious. In fact, she often had kind words to say. The only one unaffected by the magic the season change appeared to bring about was Jacob. Not even Jonah and Eliza had been able to lift him out of the depth of his despair since his meeting with the Bishop. Of course Jacob had not disclosed the reason for his mood but instead thrown himself into work. When he was forced to be in the presence of others, he ensured he had a plethora of reading material at his side as to avoid any potential conversation. The day that the warmth finally remembered their district, Jacob had been up well before dawn, milking the cows as he always did. He wanted to be done the majority of his chores before retreating to the barn and hiding in the loft. He had actually acquired an interesting mystery from the library and he was eager to read the ending. As the morning hour turned close to noon, Jacob hurried out of the chicken coop with a basket full of eggs and almost slipped in the mud near the pig pen. Steadying himself before he lost the day's yolks, he grabbed onto the fence with his free hand and looked up. Directly on the other side of the gate was the most beautiful woman he had ever seen. Her long blonde hair was loose and hanging about her gray, ankle-length dress, under a matching gray bonnet, slightly blowing in the gentle breeze. Her mouth was turned up into a crooked smile, off centered but intensely charming and as it always did, sunlight caught the molten brown of her eyes, melting the sadness out of Jacob from the moment his forlorn irises met them.

"Grace!" he whispered, hushed and looked around figuratively. "What are you doing here?"

Her beam widened.

"This is my home, Jacob, and I've come to thank you for helping me find my way back. And also I would like to inform you that my parents have painted their gate blue."

<u>Late Winter</u>

No one could have prepared her for the man standing on the other side of the door but it truly was Bishop Fisher and he was there to speak to her. Lydia had conveniently disappeared, extremely uncomfortable by the reminder of the past she had left behind but Grace had welcomed the Bishop into the cozy apartment, offering him a hot tea and they had talked for hours, about Lydia, about her parents, about why she had left and of course, about Jacob. After their discussion, the Bishop told her that he wanted to have her return but he needed to discuss it with the ministers first. Of course, the process would be long and require intense atonement for what she had done. There was one more subtlety; that she would sincerely consider Jacob as a husband. Grace had smiled and nodded. After he left, she had shaken her head and laughed. How could the Bishop know that the main reason she had wanted to return for so many years was to be with Jacob?

AMISH WISHES

JESSICA PENN

1.

Tracing her finger over the cold, gray tombstone, Joanna inhaled deeply and choked back a sob. Kneeling in the pasture of their family's cemetery, she placed a bouquet of daffodils in front of the stone. It all felt like a dream to her. She didn't think she would ever lose her mother. She was her best friend and now that she was gone Joanna felt lost. She spoke softly to the stone just as she would as if her mother were standing beside her. "Hello, Mother. I miss you more each day. I really wish you could have stayed. It's lonely here without you. Everyone is trying to be strong. They want to continue life as it was before, but without you being here, it's impossible. I know you're in a better place and you're not in pain from the illness ravaging your earthly body, but it's still hard. I just don't know what to do now. I have assumed all of your household duties, just as you would have wished, but I find myself feeling increasingly empty. None of this feels right." Before she could finish her conversation, she heard the distinctive sound of horses clopping in the distance. She knew her brothers would be coming to take her back to their small home in the center of their community. They would have finished their errands in town, and she would be needed soon to start preparing supper. Dusk would be upon them soon, and after evening services, a good meal, a nice fire, and sleep would be arriving soon.

Joanna stood up slowly and ran her fingers along the cold stone one more time, giving a weak smile of recognition to her brother, Eli, who trotted up on his prized horse, Petunia. Petunia was a gentle creature and was easily broken. Eli was good to the creature and she respected him as well, she wouldn't ever buck him off, even when they were traveling through thunderstorms or if she ran up on a snake in the tall weeds. They trusted one another. Joanna could say the same about her brother, even though she was the older sibling, they trusted one another and vowed to always protect one another through all of life's trials. Eli looked down from Petunia and frowned. He hated to see his sister suffer so, but as a young man, he knew that for the good of the community he couldn't let his own sorrows show. He had to be strong for his sister now and show nothing but unconditional support. Now was the time for them to come together as a family and keep each other close. That's what his mother would have wanted. "It's good to see you, sister. Are you ready to return to the house?"

Joanna looked up at Eli's eyes and knew that behind the deep brown spheres, there was a touch of sadness that lingered there. He was trying so hard to put on a brave front, but she knew the truth, he wouldn't be the same after their mother's passing either. "Yes. I'm ready to return, Eli. Can I ride with you?"

"Of course. I think Petunia has it in her to walk us both back home along the path." The horse merely whinnied and they both laughed at her response. As they trotted along the path, Joanna's voice turned solemn once again as she asked, "How's father today?"

"He didn't say much at all, he merely got up and went into his study, where he read some scriptures and made some notes for service, then he walked out into the garden and surveyed the crops. It was like a typical day for him it seems."

"I wish he would express himself more."

"Ah, you know how he is Joanna, that's how he always was, stoic and stone-faced."

"Yeah. Maybe one day we'll figure him out."

"Ha! You have jokes, my sister. I seriously have my doubts about that."

They rode back up to the house in relative silence only listening to the sounds of the birds chirping and the echo of Petunia's hooves against the ground. Reaching the house, the pair dismounted and Eli walked Petunia to the barn, taking care to make sure she had plenty of fresh hay and water. Joanna went straight into the house and immediately made her way to the kitchen. In her mind's eye, she could still see her mother standing by the stove, stirring a pot or leaning over to get a knife from the bottom drawer. It was up to her now to make sure the family was fed. She sighed heavily and reached up above the family's ice box to take down a larger pot which hung above it. It was cast iron and the same one that had been used in the family for generations to make hearty stews and soups. That night Joanna decided she would make the family a hearty beef stew. They had some extra meat frozen already in the icebox and she had plenty of canned vegetables from the summer and fall's gardening. She poured some water that had already been carried inside into the large cast iron pot and lit the fire beneath their wood and coal stove. When it came to a full boil she added the meat and vegetables. Her mother had always tried to make her stews last for a few days and made it a point to ensure it was filling as well. Joanna added some corn starch to thicken the broth and proceeded to flavor it with spices. When her father walked into the kitchen, he hung his head, but then looked up and met Joanna's eyes, giving her a slight nod of approval. When the preparations were finished Joanna carried the pot along with some freshly baked bread out to the dining room. The family took their assigned places around the square table. In their mourning period, it was customary to set an extra place at the table for the lost as well, so her mother's chair while empty next to her father, had a place setting and was served some stew as well. It would be her father's task to consume it.

2.

After all was seated, her father spoke. "Good evening my son and daughter. Let us all rejoice and give thanks for what the day hath brought forth. Now is the time we must graciously give thanks for the abundance the Lord hath provided us with and draw close together as a family in our hour of need. I was reading the scriptures this morning and they brought me much comfort. Despite our loss, I trust each of my children to go on living and continue to be upstanding and show true grace. Now let us break bread and honor the fallen."

They all opened their eyes and lifted their heads watching their father who broke the first bit of bread. He then passed the plate to the others who took their portions and set the tray back in the center of the table. Their meal was eaten in silence and no one dared to speak until their simple supper was finished. Their father then looked at each of them and smiled. Tufts of white hair showed his age and he had a natural ruddiness to his skin tone that made him look jovial. He also had lines etched along his forehead left by the many years of being contemplative. One would look at him and assume he was a stern man all of the time, but he had crows feet and smile lines along his eyelids that told another story. While their father was stern and quiet, Joanna could remember a time when they were children he would play their games with them and tell stories which made all of them laugh joyously. He was a man dedicated to worship, but he also was a man who prided himself on the family he had created.

Rising from the table Joanna began to gather the dishes and place them in the kitchen sink, as she crossed into the other room she heard her father say, "Joanna, I'm very pleased with all the progress you have made in the kitchen with meal preparations. Your mother, rest her soul, would be very proud of you." Tears formed in Joanna's eyes and she bit her bottom lip to choke back a sob. Her mother, Annabelle, had been gone now for over a month, but the loss still stung. Her entire family was stuck living with the reminders of her being. Joanna still hadn't had the heart to clean out her closet or her sewing room. The elders had planned a town gathering at the end of the month, however, so she thought she would take them then and donate them. After all, she was a practical woman, just like her mother before her, and knew that there was no sense in good pieces of clothing going to waste when someone less fortunate could be using them. She responded to her father when returning to the table for a second trip for the remainder of the dishes. "Thank you father, I appreciate it. I discover more techniques every day. I feel personal growth is important, don't you?"

"Why, of course it is, Joanna. I've watched you and Eli grow through the years and I'm proud of both of you. I personally feel comforted by the fact that no matter how many times I go to complete a task and fail, I always have another opportunity to give it another try. That's the beauty in salvation and forgiveness. As humans, we all fall short of perfection, but there's always the chance to redeem yourself through prayer and multiple attempts."

Eli cleared his throat and spoke for the first time since they arrived home. "I'm glad for that. I know that there have been many times I felt lost or like I was on the wrong path, but I would pray about it and then something would happen or suddenly change in my life." Joanna listened to the pair talk from the kitchen while washing up the supper dishes and smiled. She loved her father and brother dearly but felt lost. She had no one to talk about her daily affairs with now that her mother had passed. She couldn't tell her father about the gossip she overheard while getting notions for sewing. She couldn't talk to her brother about a certain feeling she had in the pit of her stomach when she watched the baker's son splitting wood while hanging their linens out to dry.

She listened as their conversation continued. Her father spoke in a good-natured tone and there was nothing condescending in his voice as he elaborated on the subject matter with his son. "Eli, do you remember that time you came home crying when you were thirteen or fourteen? It was late in the evening and mid-summer. You had just returned from Mrs. Hollister's barn dance, she was having to raise money for the local town orphanage. You came to me and had tears in your eyes and your lips were swollen and shaking. I'll never forget how dejected you looked."

"Yes, father. I remember that well. I had gone to the dance and got quite upset when I saw Pamela Davison dancing with my friend, James."

"Do you remember what I told you?"

"No, I can't say I can recall, though it must have worked, I haven't harbored feelings for Pamela since that night."

"What I told you then son, was that sometimes we think we know what's best for ourselves, but in the end, it's not us who is ultimately in control of that. Our actions may influence our day to day activities, but it is only through faith we can fulfill our ultimate destiny. Our almighty father wants us to be happy, but sometimes we have to learn a lesson the hard way so we don't pursue other things. Your courtship with Pamela, for example, is one of those things. Do you know what she's doing now?"

"No, father. I haven't a clue."

"She decided to go live among the outsiders. Her life has not been beneficial from it, given my understanding. The last news we received in a letter that she decided to pursue her career as a professional dancer. It turns out that career path led her to work in a nightclub for exotic dancing and she's developed a drug addiction. It's in my best estimation that she will more than likely spend a great deal of her life in prison for drug related crimes or prostitution. So, son, as you can see sometimes our Father doesn't answer our prayers for a reason."

"What if I could have changed her? If she stayed with me, then maybe she would have just lived her life pursuing the path of righteousness."

"Well, I know how susceptible young men are to the wiles of women and their charms. I think that given the choice, you would have left and gone with her and been corrupted by the outside world as well. Outside of our community, there is a temptation to pursue wrongdoing on every corner. No matter what your vice, there is some way to purchase it or attain it there. Never forget that on your travels, Eli."

"I won't Father."

3.

Joanna listened to their conversation while she continued to tidy up the dinner dishes. She knew that her mother would have loved that their father was attempting to socialize with his children, but she also knew that her mother would have played devil advocate in the conversation. She wasn't like most of the other women in the town. She was outspoken and often had heated debates on matters of faith or business with her father, yet they worked to balance each other out very well. Joanna was convinced that when God made her mother, his creation was done purely to spite her father and keep him in line.

She cleaned up the sink and then decided she would go ahead and get the percolator ready for the morning's coffee. She knew that would be the first thing their father would ask for when he woke up in the morning. He often preferred the strong brew first thing, then would go out to complete his chores, foregoing breakfast until their animals had been fed. He always said that if one took care of the animals, they would, in turn, take care of you. He lived by this strict routine day in and day out, with little variation in routine, save for the day he celebrated his wedding anniversary with his wife. On that day, both their father and mother would take a rare trip to town, where they would return with not only small gifts for the children but some goods, that were less costly to purchase such as new blades for the farming equipment. Joanna always dreamed of the outside world as being some type of magical realm where everyone had access to things like running water and life was easy, but as she grew older she realized the outsiders weren't much different than those in her own community. She wasn't allowed to do much traveling into town, but when she did she just noticed that the outsiders seemed to base their own value on their material belongings. This concept just simply didn't exist in her community, everything was shared.

Joanna saw that it was dark now outside and with her chores attended to, she didn't see the point in staying with the menfolk talking around the dinner table. Drying her hands on a dish towel, she decided to go ahead and excuse herself. Walking around the side of the table she approached her father and placed her hand on the side of his chair then leaned over kissing him on the forehead. "I'm going to go ahead and turn in for the evening, father. The nightly chores are all completed."

"Ah, yes, very good little one. My precious daughter. You have sweet dreams and remember that your father and brother are here if you have night terrors."

"Oh, papa. I love you. I haven't had a night terror, though, since I was seven years old."

"Still.. think good thoughts."

"I will. Goodnight. Goodnight Eli."

"Goodnight, sister, remember I love you even in your slumber."

"I will."

Joanna walked to her bedroom and lit the small candle that was on her nightstand, it provided enough light to read by, which is the only thing she enjoyed doing in the evenings to relax. Taking off her bonnet, she sat on the edge of the bed and began undoing the long braids she had in her hair. She preferred to keep it pulled up and away from her face during the course of the day since she was often doing chores. The tresses undid themselves easily and she fluffed hands through it, taking her hairbrush and running it through her long brown locks. After she put on her nightgown and hung her daytime dress back up in her standing closet, she picked up her Bible, seeing the notes she had made in the margins. She had been studying a chapter in Revelations that her father recommended. He felt that it would benefit the family to examine the reasons for death together, so they could make some sense of their mother's unexpected passing. She sighed and remembering her place decided she would finish reading and analyzing the chapter when she arose the following morning. Instead, she picked up the paperback she had borrowed from the town's library. It had a handsome cowboy on the front of it and he appeared in front of a herd of galloping horses. He was holding a blonde woman in his arms and she was swooning. Joanna smiled as the opened the book to the place she left off. It wasn't customary for women in her community to read much at all, but she enjoyed the thoughts of romance and found nothing wrong with dreaming about a handsome cowboy of her own. She finished the chapter and blew out her candle, reclining on her twin bed and closing her eyes sleeping almost immediately.

4.

As the dawn peeked through the clouds, Joanna was awakened by Eli, barging into her bedroom unannounced. He let the door bang on the hinges and had a panicked look on his face, as Joanna pulled the covers up over herself asked, "Why, Eli?! Whatever is the matter?! Is it Father?! Is he okay?!"

"Yes. Oh, Joanna, I'm worried. It's Petunia. She's fallen ill I'm afraid. Can you come out to the barn?"

Breathing out a sigh of relief, Joanna nodded and said, "Of course dear brother. Don't be fearful. The Lord will protect Petunia. Give me a few moments to get decent and I will be out there." Joanna calmly got up from her bed and walked to her closet, taking a few moments to pull her hair back and put on her bonnet then putting on her daytime dress. She pulled the laces tight on her boots and hurried out to the barn where she could see Eli standing by Petunia's stall pacing anxiously. "Thank you for coming out sister. I can't figure out what's wrong with her. She won't respond to my coaxing and she's just lethargic. I've never seen her in this state."

"Calm yourself, Eli. Your panicked state is doing her no good either. Animals can sense your fear." Joanna walked up to the mare who was laying down and looked into Petunia's deep brown eyes. She then placed her hand gently on the creature's forehead. She then stroked the animal's head and back, making soothing sounds, just as her mother would do them when they were sick youngsters. "Yes. You're right to have come to fetch me. She's definitely fallen ill. Let's just hope its a bug. Father has a trip planned to go into town to gather some new ax blades for the fall cutting. I'll go with him and stop by the library and see if I can find a cure in some of the veterinary medicine books they have shelved. Don't worry, brother. We will do what we can for her. Just be fervent in your prayers and there will be a way delivered."

Joanna walked back into the home and began preparing her father's morning coffee. Daylight had just broke and she knew he would be happy to get the day started like normal. When he walked in the kitchen he smiled seeing her standing at the stove as her mother would have, fixing his coffee and preparing breakfast for her brother. Eli always had a voracious appetite She set the steaming mug in front of him and said, "Good morning, Father. I must confess it's already been eventful."

"Oh, really how so?"

"It seems Petunia has fallen ill. I was hoping it would be okay if I went with you while you were in town today to look up some medicine for her at the library."

"I certainly hate to hear that Petunia has taken a turn for the worse. She has been good to our little family. I think that's a wonderful idea darling. God can work miracle cures, but only if we're willing to do a bit of the work as well. After the morning feeding, we will go into town. Be prepared. While I'm purchasing the new blades for the fall wood harvest, you can look into a cure for our Petunia. I bet your brother is worried sick."

"Oh, he is Father. You know he's always been close to the mare."

"We shall do what we can. Thank you for the finely brewed cup of coffee. Now I must get to work, the daylight is already streaming upon us and the chickens will be happy to receive their breakfast."

"Thank you, Father."

Joanna finished making the biscuits and gravy for breakfast then poured them all glasses of freshly squeezed orange juice from the assortment of oranges that they had traded for in town earlier in the summer. She knew their shelf life would be expiring soon and didn't want anything to go to waste. Waste not, want not, her mother always said. She also knew that they all need to keep their strength up because as soon as they got back from town the entire community would gather and chop wood for their collective heat in the winter. After completing her chores and cleaning up the cooking utensils she set the meal on the dining room table and gathered her bag for their trip into town. She made certain she had her city library card and decided to take her paperback with her and exchange it for another as it was nearing completion anyway. Looking around the empty room she sighed. She was worried about her brother, but also she felt a doubt creeping into her soul and a generalized discomfort, wondering if this is how the remainder of her days would be spent, taking care of her father and brother , never knowing the love of a man or having her own family to raise.

Her father and brother came back into the house after feeding the animals and sat down at the table, nodding in appreciation at having their meal already set before them. Eli spoke then, asking to say the morning prayers and included a blessing for his favorite mare as well. They ate the rest of their meal in silence and Joanna immediately went to the sink and began cleaning up the dishes, so she wouldn't have to do both the breakfast and dinner dishes before bed. She also was anticipating having a busy day tending to Petunia upon their return. Her father came and got her when the horses were hitched up to the wagon and her brother helped her climb in beside him. Her father gave his horses a quick pat on the head and they departed on their journey into town.

5.

Arriving in the nearest town, Joanna took in her surroundings as her father hitched up the wagon to the hitching post by the hardware store. She got out of the buggy, amidst the stares of the townspeople. She imagined she looked quite strange to then in her pale blue day dress, with her hair pinned up in a bonnet, while her father was dressed head to toe in all black, complete with his wide-rimmed black hat. His long brown beard wasn't shaved, merely groomed and it did betray his age, as spots of gray could be seen in it when the sun hit it just right. He spoke briefly to his daughter before going inside the store. "Remember daughter, be polite to the townspeople, but do not engage in lengthy conversation unless it pertains to spreading the Gospel. I will be here when you are ready to leave but try to find the information you seek quickly. I suspect this lost time will hurt our productivity later and we won't be able to get as much done as we should. Be careful, Joanna."

Joanna nodded and hugged her father before crossing the street and rounding the block heading to the library. She cast her eyes downward mostly only looking up periodically to dodge obstacles. She opened the doors to the city library and the pleasant librarian smiled and waved at her when she entered. She smiled back and returned the greeting. She liked the librarian, who never questioned her when she came in even as a little girl clutching her mother's skirts. The older clerk would give her lollipops when her mother checked out her religious books and romance novels. Now Joanna was grown and even though she didn't get a lollipop, she still felt those warm feelings when she was in the library. She walked up to the desk and quietly dropped her book on the counter. "I need to return this, and I will be getting another one if I can find the other information I need in time."

"Sure thing, Joanna. Have you been doing okay, since your mother's passing?"

"Oh, yes we have been doing alright, thank you. I'm sorry I was in such a bad state when you saw me last. I am adjusting to this new normal."

"Well, that's good. If you need anything, you let me know as always."

"I will. I will see you when I return."

Joanna then walked off, smiling once more at the clerk. She rounded the corner to the reference desk where there was no clerk, but there was a younger looking man in grease-stained coveralls standing by the finance books, looking bewildered. Joanna watched him pull out a book from the shelf as the rest came tumbling down. She couldn't stifle a small giggle as he fumbled trying to catch them all. He turned around hearing her laughter and she was met with a sheepish smile and the most striking blue eyes she'd ever seen. He took her by surprise as she felt her heart beat faster within her chest and suddenly heat rose to her face as she blushed deeply. Before she could say a word he smiled broadly at her and said, "They don't make these shelves the way they used to do they?"

Joanna giggled once again and said, "No. They certainly don't."

"I don't really know much about this place. I needed a book on taxes, I own my own mechanic shop and I'm doing my own this year to save money for the business. Maybe I should have just paid someone."

"Well, what are you looking for? Maybe I can help."

"A book to tell me how to do it."

Joanna paused for a moment surveying the shelves then reached down to the bottom one, accidently brushing the man's hand as she picked up a hefty volume and placed it in his arms. "Here you go. This will guide you through the process."

"Oh wow. Thank you. I appreciate that ma'am. It's nice to meet you, my name's David."

"I'm Joanna. I'm not from around here, as you can tell."

David took a step toward her, closing the distance, and Joanna felt a certain electricity pass through them. She let the heat rise to her cheeks again and once more looked into his blue eyes. He was in good shape and looked strong from his work. He had blonde hair and was clean shaven. He didn't look like any of the men from their community, but he did seem to possess the same kindness behind his eyes and good spirit. He responded by saying, "I wish you were from around here. I'd hire you to do my taxes."

She chuckled at his joke, then suddenly remembered her purpose. "I really hate to cut on conversation short, David, but I have to get some information then return to my community, my brother's horse is sick and needs medical attention I know nothing of."

"Oh, I'm sorry to hear that. Maybe I can help. I grew up on a ranch."

She couldn't believe her ears. She had wanted a cowboy all of her own. Could it be that her prayers had been answered? He seemed so genuine and caring. She explained the problem with Petunia and David gave her the information she needed to attend to the mare. He reassured her it was nothing major that some tender loving care couldn't fix. He then went on to say that his specialty in life was fixing broken things. Joanna considered the gravity of his statement before turning to leave and decided to do something she would need to ask forgiveness for later.

"You have been so helpful David, could I have your address?"

"Only if I can have yours too."

The pair exchanged addresses and Joanna exited the library, turning around to see David staring at her making her exit. She didn't know what had come over her, but she knew in her heart this man was her destiny.

6.

She exited the library to find her father standing red-faced by the door, checking his pocket watch. She hadn't realized how much time had passed talking with David, she only knew that it felt like they had known each other a lifetime. Feeling the need to apologize she spoke to her father, when they crossed to the buggy, "I'm sorry, father. It took me longer to get the information I needed than what I thought."

He didn't say anything, but merely nodded and coaxed the horses out of the lot and towards the path back to their community. Her father finally spoke when they were close to the halfway point between town and their village. "You know why we caution each other when talking with townspeople? It's not because our religion has restrictions on being social and making friends. In fact, we are encouraged to witness to everyone we possibly can. It's because not all people are righteous, Joanna. Not everyone will have your best interest at heart, and the original evil does find its way into the hearts of men. Some of the people you encounter in the outside world, well let's say the majority of them, only are interested in preying on the weak. It's their life's goal, not helping others or doing good."

Joanna turned her eyes downward again as her father patted her on the leg continuing, "Remember, no matter what happens, Joanna, your family will always support you within the community. We, however, could not help you should you decide to live among the outsiders. You would be shunned and on your own, you know it's our way, there's no changing that." Joanna nodded in acknowledgment, silently rubbing the piece of paper in her pocket which had David's address on it. She knew in her heart, that she needed to see the mysterious cowboy mechanic once again, but didn't like the idea of her father's disapproval. He would never allow such a thing, she felt conflicted and sick at heart the entire way home.

Arriving back at the community they were greeted by Eli, whose worried look had only grown more exasperated during their time away. "Greetings, Father. Greetings, Sister. Did you acquire the knowledge you sought?"

"I did brother. Let's go to the barn and see what we can do."

Together they walked to the barn and checked on Petunia. Joanna took care to follow David's precise instructions and administered a careful mixture of salt brine and water to the mare who greedily lapped it up. It had seemed that she had just gotten a bit dehydrated during their previous days' activities and was feeling under the weather. They monitored her condition throughout the day and it did improve as she eventually got up and started wandering back and forth in her stall, anxious for a trot. In addition to that the new blade purchase, expedited the wood cutting process and the community made short work of the wood pile, stockpiling enough wood to last the entire winter in half the time it normally would. They decided as a community to celebrate their recent accomplishment and give thanks to the Lord, with a feast to be held that upcoming Saturday night.

Joanna spent the night quietly in her room after supper and allowed herself to think of David. She knew beyond a shadow of a doubt that she needed him in her life. She believed, despite her father's warnings that there were good and decency in his soul. No one without a good heart, would have freely given her that information she needed to help her animal. Most of the outsiders would have offered their services and charged a pretty penny for such knowledge. Joanna thought of the feast Saturday and sighed. Did she want to be stuck in the community all her life, eventually marrying a man who had little passion for anything in life? It was then Joanna made her decision. She would slip away during the barn dance on Saturday and go see David.

As the community was abuzz with the festivities at the dance on Saturday night, Joanna excused herself to go back to the house, hugging her brother and her father tightly before exiting, saying she felt ill and needed to call it an early night. Unnoticed by anyone else in the community, she then proceeded down the well-worn path and made her way to town. She made her way to the address David had scrawled on a ripped piece of an envelope from his coveralls and knocked on his door.

David opened the door, rubbing his eyes, apparently awakened by her rapping. He was groggy but smiled broadly in recognition. "Joanna, is that you are am I dreaming?"

"No. You're not dreaming, David. I'm really here." She paused a moment, considering her options. She thought for a moment about what advice her mother would give her in this moment. She thought back to when she was a little girl clutching on to her mother's skirt, frightened by some imaginary threat. She would have said, "Ah, my precious little girl, there is nothing to be afraid of but your own imagination. If you don't give your fear power over you, you can achieve anything you want in this lifetime." Joanna hesitated a moment then said to David all while blushing and smiling, "I came to be with you David, and hopefully one day be your wife."

David took Joanna by the hand and led her over his front stoop, making sure she didn't trip over the door sill on the way in. When he shut the door behind her he pulled her into his arms and kissed her deeply. Joanna felt a joy like none other she had felt in her life, spread through her bones and body. He then looked deeply into her eyes and said, "Well. I'm not the smartest man you will ever know, nor will I ever be the ideal of perfection, but I promise you this Joanna. I am a decent man with a good heart, and I promise to make this life the best we can possibly have together. So, yes. I do want you to stay with me. You're all I've thought about since I met you that day at the library, and you're all I want to think about for the rest of my days." The pair then walked hand in hand into David's modest living room where they sit side by side on the sofa, holding each other until they drifted off peacefully.

amish awakening

TORI WOODS

Chapter 1

Hannah stood at the window of her classroom looking out towards the green landscape that stretched out as far as she could see, dark clouds started gathering and was drawing closer with each passing minute. To most those clouds were a sign of new life, but to her it bore nothing but bad memories she simply chose to forget. Father Smith often told her that in order to find peace within herself she would need to make peace with herself, but how could she if it wasn't herself she was angry at? It wasn't her fault that Aaron died.

"Hanna, will you be fine to get home before the storm gets here?" Kemp asked as popping his head in at the class.

Kemp had been a good friend for her, since Aaron's death he had taken it upon himself to be the man of the house, but as Aaron's younger sibling, she felt awkward knowing that he wanted more from her. He may not have said it out loud but his constant fussing over her wellbeing said enough.

"I'll be fine, thank you Kemp, I'm having supper with Father Smith and his family," she said and offered him a friendly smile.

"Of course, well you be careful now," Kemp said and hesitated before turning to leave.

Hannah let out a soft sigh and sent up a silent prayer of thanks. She was growing weary trying to be nice all the time by courteously ignoring Kemp's advances, but some days she itched to just be blatantly rude and tell him to stop trying. But that will cause a few frowns to furrow on the elders' brows. She waited until Kemp was out of sight before she grabbed her basket with her books and left the single structured school building that housed no more than thirty four school children ranging from all ages.

She hurried along the road to get home but the storm was drawing closer faster than expected. Another perfect day ruined, she thought as she treaded ahead, keeping a watchful eye on the clouds rolling in and as the first drops started plummeting down on her she quickened her pace. The sound of rolling thunder droned in her ears and she clutched her basket tighter, but when an automobile pulled up next to her she realized it was not thunder.

"You won't make it far at this pace *lieb*," the very familiar yet disembodied voice of the driver spoke from inside the car.

"*Lieb*? It is a bad habit making such a personal reference to complete stranger," she said to the man and stepped closer to get a better look at her assailant or her rescuer.

"Greetings Hannah, it's been a long time."

Hannah froze; it was Mason who sat before her as big as life, in an automobile of all things. The last time she had seen him was when she was just seventeen. He had always been the black sheep in the community, disobeying so many of the rules, that by the time he turned eighteen he decided to venture into the great big modern world, and disappeared from her life.

"Mason Smith," she said and smiled, "you have not changed one bit."

He threw his head back and laughed, "In this light you cannot see my grey hairs. Now are you going to walk the rest of the way home, or will you let me take you."

She swayed and looked down at her feet, contemplating a ride. She was sure that it will just loosen a few tongues if she arrived home with him.

"*Denki*, but I think I will walk, it's not too far now," she declined and stepped away from the automobile, "I'm sure to see you at your father's house?"

Mason smiled and nodded at her, "That depends if my father will welcome me into his house."

"The Prodigal son returns," she said raising her shoulders and tucking them forward as the rain started to pelt down around her, "I'll see you later."

Instead of running along the road, she chose to run across the fields towards her house and away from Mason. Seeing him after all these years should not have caused such a kaleidoscope of butterflies to wreak havoc in her stomach but it has. She had noticed the slight grey hair peppered against his temples and the increased amount of laughing lines that deepened next to his eyes when he smiled. He had also no beard, which meant that he had not yet been wed, but then again, the modern worlds' cultures are far different to their own simple way of life, and the mere thought left her wondering where he had been all these years.

By the time she reached her house, she was completely drenched right through to her undergarments. She suddenly felt nervous to attend supper with the Smiths' but unless she was ill she could not come up with an honest enough excuse as to why she can't attend. She was going to have to just try and act as normal as possible around Mason, that is if his father allows him to sit with them.

Chapter 2

Mason left the community just after his eighteenth birthday, and the day he left, his father told him that he would wait for him. Personally he never thought he would come back here, but life has the tendency to throw curveballs when least expected. And from personal experience the curve balls just keep coming.

He hardly expected to see Hannah, or rather he expected that she would still be here, but he didn't expect their run in with each other to have such an effect on him. Even when he approached her from a distance, his gut told him that it was Hannah walking alongside the road. Call it providence or pure chance, but he would recognize her from every angle simply by the way she walked. She had this distinct way of walking on her toes while hardly moving her arms. Now years after experiencing the modern world, her walk reminded him a ballerina, precise and delicately calculated and all his memories came flooding back.

When she ran across the field he couldn't help but smile, knowing that she too had a moment of dejavu and for a moment he silently wished he never left, but he knew if he did stay it would have been for her only and he simply could not tie himself down to a life of common needs and simplicity, he was too eager to explore the world.

As he pulled up to his fathers' house he looked up at the house, as usual well kept, but a simple uncomplicated structure, like their way of life here in Lancaster. He remembered his life here as if it was yesterday, and although he had an enquiring and curious mind, he had to admit that staying here would have prevented many complications in his life. His cell phone vibrated on his dash but he chose to ignore it, instead he shoved it in the glove compartment and got out of the car.

"Mason!" his mother cried out as she came running down the stairs hugging him tight.

His father stood at the stop of the stairs with his arms crossed and a deadpan expression that would put a corpse to shame, but then again his father was never one to show any emotion unless it was to hand out corporal punishment and of that he had more than his fair share.

"*Mamm*, it's good to see you," he said and hugged his mother. She had gotten old and although she appeared relaxed he could see that life and labour had taken its toll.

"Mason my son, please come inside, we are so happy to have you here," his mother said excitedly.

"*Daed*, how are you?" he asked his father boldly.

"We're fine, ya," his father responded flatly and stood aside for him to enter.

Nothing had changed since he initially left for his Rumspringa, which he never returned from, and being back after so many years, was like a time traveling experience.

"Lydia is married now," his mom said as she set a space for him at the dinner table.

"I know, she wrote me."

His mother and father exchanged looks and then went on as if he never said a word.

"She's with child, and the baby should be here within the month or so."

Clearly his father did not approve of his sister writing to him, so instead he smiled, "I will make an effort to congratulate her when I see her."

The awkward silence was followed with a light knock and when he turned around to see who it was, he was pleasantly surprized to find Hannah standing in the doorway.

"Mason, Hannah has dinner with us every Friday evening," his mother said and gestured for Hannah to sit down.

Mason turned to her, "Do you not have a family of your own?"

"Let's say grace," Mason's father interrupted and he immediately could have kicked himself for asking such a personal question. Now that he was back among his family he had to be careful of what he said and how he said things.

They all took hands and while his father said grace, Mason was acutely aware of Hannah's hand in his. He could feel her fingers trembling in his and he smiled. He made her nervous; he could only hope it was the good kind of nervous.

After dinner they all sat at the table while Hannah and Mrs Smith gathered the dishes and took it to the kitchen.

"How long are you planning on visiting?" Mason's father asked.

"Not sure, at the moment it's indefinitely."

A loud crash sounded from the kitchen, and his father's intense gaze held his.

"Indefinitely is a long time."

"Depending on the inevitability of it," Mason said.

"You're room is still as it was, your mother never changed it. She waited for you."

"At least someone did."

He held his father's gaze and then stood up and excused himself. He had to give his father time; he had been away for such a long time, with little or no contact. But then again if they were just a little bit more open minded towards the use of modern technology he would have been in constant contact with his family. The few letters he exchanged with his sister was hard enough to keep up with, as it stands, people no longer wrote letters and wasted their time with postage, they e-mailed or chatted to each other.

"I'll get my things from the car," Mason said and excused himself from the table.

Chapter 3

Hannah spent the entire evening seated next to Mason trying her best not to breathe, or inhale the intoxicating smell that filled her nostrils every time he moved. The odd time she visited town she often took a sneaky sniff of the perfumes that were sold, more to remind her just how much power there was in such an evil cheap substance, or so she told herself. But now here next to Mason, the smell turned from offensive to hallucinogenic. Every time she found herself leaning towards him and then she had to recite a bible verse that reminded her of infidelity and the sinful nature of the flesh. I shall not want, she kept saying to herself mentally and when Mrs Smith got up and started to clear the table, she was only too thankful to join her and get away from the magnetic pull that was threatening to ruin her.

That was until she heard Mason mention that his stay was indefinite. That meant she was going to see him every single day until he decides to run away again.

The words came as such a shock that she dropped the plate she was holding. Mrs Smith was quick to bend down and help her pick up the broken pieces.

"He has changed," she said to Hannah, "but he's still my son."

"The world tends to change a person," Hannah whispered and smiled at the older woman with the sad blue eyes.

She remembered the day they realized Mason was not going to come back, his mother was in tears for days, while his father put up this façade of callous indifference. But she knew they missed their son.

"Hannah, you can make him see the truth."

That was a tall order; Hannah thought and tossed the glass into the bin.

"I don't think it is my place to convince him," she said.

"You're right I'm sorry, I just – I don't want him to leave again."

Hannah could understand how Mason's mother must have felt, for someone to leave for such a long time is almost like sending someone off to the beyond. But how was she going to convince him to stay, he had experienced the modern world and drove an automobile not to mention that he used men's perfume. Why would he trade that freedom for this?

"I think I need to head home Mrs Smith, I still have a quilt to finish before Sunday," she said and gathered her coat, "I'll be seeing you."

"Of course dear, but do come around when you want some company."

"I sure will."

Hannah was tucked under her blanket in front of the fireplace and had just started to quilt when there was a slight knock on the door. What a strange time for a visitor, she thought as she went to open the door.

"Mason," she said shocked.

"Hannah, may I come in?"

"I-I don't think it's proper for me to invite you in," she said and reached for her shawl, and then stepped outside, closing the door behind her.

"I understand, I just thought you could use some company," he said with a smile that tugged at the corners of his mouth.

She felt her stomach tumble again and she took a deep steadying breath.

"We can go for a walk," she offered.

"Sure." Mason held out his arm but instead she wrapped her arms around herself.

"Why did you come back?"

"It's a long story."

One he would most likely not want to share with her, but she was curious as to why he was back. What if he was running from the law, she thought slightly panicked, but she couldn't see him to be someone who would use this community as a curtain to hide behind.

"We'll time is what I have. You left here in such a hurry, and now after I don't know even how long, you're back like a ghost from the past."

"Maybe I am a ghost, and I decided to come and haunt you," he said and laughed.

Hannah also laughed and shook her head, "A lot has changed since you left."

"Like what, a few more babies born and a few sad souls sent to the hereafter? Come on Hannah, nothing changes amongst the Amish, you know that."

"Well I got married," she said and when he stopped she turned to look at him.

"And you're here walking with me, what will your husband have to say?"

"He's no longer here; he passed away," *and I'm grateful he did*, she thought not voicing her true feelings. What would Mason have said if he knew Aaron's true colours?

"So who was he?"

"Who was who?"

"Your husband, who was the lucky guy?"

"Aaron."

An awkward silence settled between them and Hannah bit her lip. Even when they were teenagers, Mason and Aaron always competed to gain her attention. They were the trio of friends who did everything together as kids, and as they got older she always thought she would marry Mason the day they were old enough. But the day Mason left he broke her heart, she waited for him to return but he never did and eventually she gave in and married Aaron, thinking they would have a happy life. But Aaron wasn't the same fun loving boy she knew or maybe he knew all along that he was just a plaster for her broken heart, a replacement for Mason, which is why he was so angry with her all the time.

"Was he good to you?" Mason asked as if he could read her mind.

"He was a good man," she responded averting her eyes.

"That was not my question Hannah," he said and took her by the shoulders, "was he good to you?"

In the moonlight she could see the flecks of silver in his blue eyes, and her heart ached with longing. But this was not right, no matter what her heart and body wanted, in her mind she was determined that she would not lust after another man. Yes she was a widow and yes, she may remarry, but that thought had never crossed her mind. Only now with Mason back she had dabbled with the idea of having her happily ever after, but it was only a dream. Just like the dream she had when she was only sixteen. And from experience all dreams eventually fade and turn into a cruel reality.

She pulled away from him and turned around to head back to the house.

"I do not wish to discuss Aaron with you," she blurted out as she felt tears sting her eyes, "Go home Mason, your mother will be worried about you."

Chapter 4

Mason had this strange feeling that Aaron had turned out to be exactly what he always thought. As young men they both loved Hannah, and although they never showed it in the open there was a sort of rivalry between them. The day he decided to go on a Rumspringa, Aaron had thanked him for leaving, and Mason had felt as if he had betrayed Hannah, but Aaron was also his friend and at the time he figured he'll be the lesser one and allow his friend a fair chance, hoping that Hannah will calm the anger in Aaron. Aaron was your average young man, but he had an angry and cruel disposition, when no-one was watching he was the one who threw stones at new born lambs and shot birds out of the trees with a sling shot, simply for the fun of it. Even his mother had to deal with his insubordination, but in front of the rest of the community he was the son everyone wished for.

Mason felt a cold stab of regret at the thought of Aaron hurting Hannah and knowing that he was indirectly to blame, made him feel sick. He had to find out what she had gone through and try and fix what he had broken, but with the hands of time waiting for no one, he wouldn't even know where to start, or whether it was too late for a new beginning.

He set off after Hannah as she rushed back to the house.

"Hannah wait!" he called but she didn't turn, she just walked straight ahead.

"Hannah!"

"Go home Mason," she said sternly but as she reached for the door handle he placed his hand over hers.

"Did he hurt you?"

He felt her back straighten and her entire body go rigid, her actions confirming his suspicions.

"Oh my god, I'm so sorry," he said and squeezed her shoulder with his other hand.

She turned in his arms and her eyes were cold and hard as she looked at him.

"Do not use the Lords name in vain."

Right, he was among very religious people now, he had to count his words and check his actions all the time.

"I'm sorry, it's a bad habit, but I am truly sorry," he said and then pulled her in to hug her.

"Mason, please," he heard her plead against his chest, "why don't you go back to where you came from?"

Was she so mad at him that she wanted him to leave? He knew he probably didn't deserve her time but surely she could understand that they were all young and he was curious about the world. She could have gone with him when he asked her but she was too scared to set foot outside of this protected cocoon of a life she was too familiar with.

"That's not happening in a hurry sweetheart," he said and tilted her chin up, "I'm here to stay, for a while."

When she looked up at him he was tempted to kiss her, but instead he took a step back.

"I'll be seeing you at Church on Sunday," he said and then tipped his hat and made his way home.

He had to keep reminding himself that life amongst the Amish wasn't anything like the world out there; he had to watch his tongue and try his best not to be tempted by a beautiful woman. As it were, temptation had caused him enough headaches to last him a life time.

He looked at his phone and grimaced. Roxanne had been phoning him non-stop, and he had no desire to return her calls and if he had a penny left he would pay her to go away. She deceived him, made him believe she was in love with him, and then tricked him into making him believe she was with child. He had found out by chance that she was lying to him, and when he did it was the last straw. It was that, which finally made him realize that the world he had chosen to embrace was nothing but a place where people are self-centred and illogical. None of his worldly friends or rather foes knew where he was, he had also turned off his location based service on his phone in case anyone wanted to track him down.

If he was going to make a change and revert back to the old ways of the Amish, he was going to have to consider getting rid of his electronic devices, but he wasn't so sure if he was willing to part with his music. That was the one thing he had grown to enjoy about life on the outside, while here amongst the Amish musical instruments were forbidden.

Chapter 5

A week has passed since Mason's arrival in Lancaster, and Hannah had done everything in her power to avoid him. Not because she disliked him or because she was angry with him, but because he stirred emotions she had completely forgotten about. She spent hours on her knees praying that the Lord take away the feelings that she harboured.

She glanced at herself in the mirror once again and sighed. Why does she even bother about her appearance, it was not like her to be so vain, but she's spent more time in front of the mirror in the past week than she did in her entire life. She rolled her plated hair into a bun and pinned it to her head before putting on her bonnet, she had to get over this stupid notion that there could be anything between her and Mason. He was a confused man with a foot in both worlds, and if he was not able to decide where he belonged how was she going to fit into his world anyway. Tonight she was going to be attending the sing, and she knew for a fact that Mason would be there too. Her stomach tumbled again and she clutched the front of her dress and sighed heavily. The sooner she got this over with the better, but as she exited the house, he was waiting for her. He had borrowed his father's buggy and was even wearing traditional Amish clothes.

"I was about to come and find you," he said and smiled.

"You wouldn't have had to look far."

"Indeed, you look beautiful."

Hannah felt her cheeks flame up and she quickly looked down and cleared her throat. Why after all these years did he still have this effect on her?

"Thank you."

"Can I offer you a ride to the Sing?"

"I was- I was going to take a walk, I enjoy the fresh air," she lied and shifted her weight.

"Are you going to avoid me for the rest of your life?"

"I don't know what you mean."

"You avoided me at church service; you hide in your class room every day. I'm not a bad man Hannah," he said and came to stand before her.

"I'm not avoiding you, I'm a busy woman," *and dead scared that the feelings I have will be unrequited,* she thought.

"Lying is as great a sin as blasphemy, so why don't you tell me why you are avoiding me?"

Hannah rolled her eyes and stepped past him, "We're going to be late, and I don't have time for idle chit chat."

"We're not going anywhere until you tell me what you are afraid of," he insisted and caught her arm.

She felt a shiver run down her spine as his hand wrapped around her upper arm, and although her sleeve offered some resistance it still felt as if his fingers were touching her bare skin.

Should she tell him what really scared her, and admit to him that she still had feelings for him despite the fact that she had given herself to Aaron all those years ago? Should she tell him how Aaron took his anger outbursts out on her and caused her to lose their child? The day she was promised to Aaron her nightmare started, although she could not deny him physically she hated every intimate moment with him. He took what he wanted when he wanted, and if she wasn't responsive enough he would get physically abusive with her. It took her a good few years to finally get over her fears and make peace with what had happened. The community never spoke a word about it although they all knew, and even when the elders got involved nothing was done.

"Get in the buggy, I'll take you to the sing," he said and led her to the carriage.

"It's not appropriate," she said and tugged her arm free.

"We're adults, not teenagers," he said and then softened his tone, "It's just a ride to my father's house."

She sighed and then got into the buggy, with her hands folded tightly on her lap.

The drive to the sing was cloaked in complete silence, and it felt as if she was suffocating with words that were trying to force their way up in her throat. She had to just get through this evening and keep calm, she kept telling herself, but she knew that it was not going to be that easy. Mason kept looking at her and she could feel his gaze rest on her face.

"Staring at me is not going to change anything," she said and looked directly at him. If he wasn't going to get the hint she was going to have to be honest with him.

He pulled the carriage to a halt and turned to her and unexpectedly cupped her face and pressed his lips against hers. For a moment she froze as his lips pressed against hers, then suddenly that intoxicated musky scent filled her senses. Her defences weakened instantly and she willingly parted her lips, but as his tongue touched hers she pulled away and jumped out of the buggy and ran.

"Lord, forgive me, I have sinned," she prayed and rushed across the field towards the Smiths' house. How could she have been so weak to allow a man to seduce her? But even as guilt flooded her, she kept thinking of his kiss and memories of a long time ago flooded her mind.

The day before he left he had kissed her, not like he kissed her tonight, but it was a kiss that remained with her all these years. A kiss she tucked away in the confines of her mind, and now that, that memory had resurfaced she felt confused and uncertain.

By the time she got to the Sing, Mason's carriage was already there. She composed herself as much as she could before entering the house. He was nowhere to be seen, but the house was full of young eager teenagers, happily singing their songs of worship. Although the event had nothing to do with devotion it was one of the more sociable events, where all the young people normally got to socialize.

She made her way through to the kitchen and joined the older women where they were preparing food.

"Did Mason fetch you?" Mrs Smith asked as she came to stand next to Hannah.

"He did come around, but I walked here instead," she said softly.

"He fancies you Hannah," she said as she moved closer, almost whispering.

"I know, I just don't know if it's appropriate. He hasn't been among us for so long and people will talk."

"You're a widow, Aaron is gone and I can guarantee you that no one will be raising any brows at you."

Hannah sighed, if it wasn't Mason it was his mother, but she knew that someone in the community would have something to say about such a union.

During the sing, Hannah was intensely aware of Mason's presence, but what made it worst was that Kemp was also there, and it suddenly felt like a bad case of dejavu with a very familiar love triangle forming, but Kemp was not aware of Mason's intent. Sooner or later he was going to realize it and then she would be stuck in the middle.

Before the sing was over, she snuck out, hoping that she left undetected, but her luck had run out.

"Hannah," it was Kemp who fell into step beside her, "You're leaving so early, are you not feeling well?"

"Oh no, I'm fine, I'm just a little tired."

She was lying again, she was going to go straight to hell at this rate, she thought to herself.

"Let me get the carriage and I'll take you home."

"No!" she all but shouted, and then toned her voice down, "I mean, no thank you. I'd rather walk."

The look on Kemp's face was one of concern but he didn't push, he simply smiled, "I'll keep you company then."

She was growing weary with this whole avoiding men thing, at this point she felt as if she was a lamb being cornered by a pack of wolves and she hated every minute of it. On the one hand Kemp was a nice man, the complete opposite of Aaron, but he was just too familiar to her. And then there was Mason, who she had feelings for since the age of fourteen. This was all too much.

"Hannah, we've known each other for a long time, and I was thinking we should consider a future together," he said out of the blue.

"Uh-I, I'm not sure I understand?"

"I want to marry you," Kemp said without blinking.

If she had a mouth full of food, she would have choked right this minute. This was a little sudden, and she knew why he had moved so quickly, he must feel threatened with Mason back in town.

"Kemp, you're a wonderful man, but I don't see a future with you, we've had too much history and having been married to Aaron makes it awkward."

"How so?" he asked as he took her hand in his.

She pulled her hand away, "It just does, if I was to marry again, it would be for love and what we have is just a friendship, which I value."

The disappointment on his face saddened her, but she could not lie and pretend that she saw a future with him. She stood and watched as he finally walked away from her before she continued to her house, but as she reached her door, Mason appeared out of the shadows.

"So it's Kemp?" he asked blankly.

"Excuse me?"

"Kemp, you wouldn't even allow me to take you to the sing because you don't want him to see you with me."

"First of all, it is not Kemp, we are just friends and secondly the reason I walked to the sing was because you kissed me. You had no right," she said angrily.

"You enjoyed that kiss as much as I did, why do you deny it?"

Hannah unlocked her door and then turned to Mason, "This is not a forsaken place like the city Mason, we have values, I have values and if you cannot respect that then there is no place for you here."

Mason approached her and stopped so close she could inhale his very breath.

"Do you have feelings for me, because if you don't, I need to know and stop wasting my time."

"Why? It's not as if you're planning on staying here, you'll leave just like you did all those years ago and I'm sorry Mason, but I will not subject myself to such disappointment again."

She didn't wait for his response simply entered the house and shut the door behind her. Regardless of the condition of her heart, she was not going to leave it out in the open to be trampled on again. The ball was in his court now, if he really was interested in her. He would have to prove himself.

Chapter 6

Mason spent a week contemplating his future, and every time he saw Hannah, he was more and more convinced that he would not leave a second time, and after consulting with his father and the other elders, they agreed to baptize him into the church. He may have been gone longer than most, but he was never officially shunned from the community. And regardless of his life style in the city, they opted to overlook his error in judgement.

It was a private affair with only the elders and his close family around to witness the baptism, and once it was over, he decided to go to the school and wait for Hannah. When she exited the school his heart skipped a beat, it was quite strange how his own emotions were suddenly so intensified after the baptism, he had often wondered if this baptism really changed anyone, but now he knew beyond the shadow of a doubt he was a new person. He had died down his old life and was willing to walk the straight and narrow with Hannah by his side if she let him.

"Afternoon Hannah," he said as she reached him.

"Mason, what brings you here?"

He smiled and took his hat off, "I wanted to come see you."

She smiled and tucked a lose strand of hair behind her ear, "Is that so?"

Even Hannah looked different now, it was as if this cloud of fog that kept skewed his outlook on life had been lifted, "Yes indeed, would you like to go for a walk with me?"

He saw her hesitate slightly but then she nodded, "Of course, I could use some fresh air before I have to go to the sisters meeting."

They walked in silence for a short while and as if they were both searching for words they spoke at the exact same time, "I wanted...." Mason started.

"What did you..." Hannah interrupted and then giggled.

"Well, it spent some time thinking about what you said."

Bending down he picked a small yellow flower and then handed it to her, "I have decided to stay here in Lancaster. My father was willing to baptize me so I'm once again part of the community."

The look on her face was priceless, and the way her eyes lit up made him want to kiss her there and then, but he refused to ruin a perfect moment.

"You did?" she asked breathlessly.

"Yes, you see, I left here thinking that the world was what I needed, and for some time it was fun, but after I returned here and saw you again, I realized what a big mistake that was."

He could tell she didn't know what to say by the way her mouth fell opened and closed, so he continued, "Hannah, I know a lot has happened and you're afraid of commitment, but I've always loved you and I want to spend the rest of my life proving that to you."

"Mason..." she started and looked down at the flower in her hand, "what if you decide to leave again?"

"I won't, my life is here now, my family and friends, and I want to be where you are." He stepped closer and cupped the side of her face, "Only if that is what you want."

Hannah leaned into his touch and a single tear ran down the side of her cheek which he wiped with the pad of his thumb.

"Do you promise to stay?" she asked in a trembling voice.

"I promise."

"Good because my heart would never survive if you broke it a second time," she said and walked into his arms.

"I'll protect it with my life."

****

Four months later, Hannah and Mason finally got married. Mason had laid down his former life and found his own feet amongst his fellow Amish folk, but he would never have been able to do this without Hannah. She was his beacon in his dark night.

AMISH SUNSET

NANCY MANN

Chapter I

Rain decorated the grassy fields of Lancaster County. The sky was a cloud grey, the sun remaining absent as the county mourned for the loss of William Bradshire, a carpenter that had been known throughout the county for his kindness and love towards the people around him.

Friends and family had gathered in the county's cemetery for William's funeral, one of the mourners being William's love, Mary Lee Warner. Out of everyone there, Mary was the most damaged from it. William's parents had passed on early in his life due to illnesses and the remaining family he had weren't as close. If anything, Mary was the only one there who truly was family to him.

As Bishop David spoke about his memories with William, Mary thought to herself how God could do such a thing, to take away an innocent being this early in his life. William was only in his mid-twenties, like Mary. He had so much to experience in his life, but it was stripped away from him so early due to the accident.

"If anyone has anything to say, speak now." Bishop David said, stepping back and letting anyone step forward to speak.

There was a long pause, silence being present as Mary thought to herself. Eventually, she took a step forward, standing in front of the casket as she let out a depressed sigh.

"William...had a beautiful soul," Mary said quietly, holding onto a wildflower, "a soul that I have yet to find in any other human being."

Everyone was watching her speak, seeing what Mary had in her hand and what she had to say about William being gone.

"I can't imagine not meeting him in my life...all the memories we've made together...all the laughter, the love...I'm going to miss it." Mary spoke as tears ran down her cheeks. "I don't know if I will find another William in my life."

Some of William's family members began to have tears fall too as they listened to Mary's words about their lost kin. Mary soon stepped back from the casket, having finished speaking on the behalf of William's death. Bishop David soon stepped forward again, wiping some tears from his own eyes.

"Thank you Mary...I will say, before I close in prayer, that it will be difficult to find another William in our lives." Bishop David said to Mary before opening his Bible.

Verses from the Bible were soon spoken out loud, everybody bowing their heads in prayer as Bishop David spoke. While everyone listened, Mary wasn't listening to the verses, in fact, she was in her own mind at this point.

"Why God...why would you take William away from me?" Mary thought to herself. *"William didn't even get half way into his life...why would you take him now?"*

As she struggled with the idea of William passing on, Bishop David finished reading the verses, quietly speaking the word *amen* as he closed his Bible, everybody soon leaving the scene of the funeral, letting the casket to be lowered into the grave. While the casket lowered, Mary was the only one present, witnessing her love's final presence on the surface of Earth.

In regards to funeral traditions of the Amish, flowers were not placed on the casket. For Mary though, traditions meant nothing to her in this occasion. She took the wildflower that she was holding in her hand and tossed it down into the undug grave, letting it land on the coffin before the gravediggers began to bury the coffin.

"I love you so much William." Mary said as the coffin soon disappeared from the soil piling on top. Tears continued to fall onto the soil as she left the site of the funeral.

Chapter II

Several years later...the county had returned back to its normal ways, except for Mary. Ever since William passed away, Mary wasn't her old self. Her old cheerful personality had passed on as well, leaving her a closed up, emotionless woman in her mid-twenties.

She tried to return back to a normal life by going to church, seeing if God might be able to help her find peace, but the more she went the church, the more she began to question God. At times, she would find herself being angry at God for taking William away this early in his life. Eventually, Mary stopped going to church, which brought the concern of Bishop David, leading him to go to Mary's home.

Her house was a little way from town, being near one of the farms. She lived in a large house that belonged to William and his parents. Now that William passed on, Mary now owned the house and lived in it by herself.

Bishop David knocked on the front door, waiting for it to be opened. It took a few knocks before the door finally opened, Mary standing there in a stone grey dress.

"Yes?" Mary quietly said, looking at him with her expressionless face.

"May I come in?" Bishop David asked softly, his expression being hopeful that she would accept his request.

Mary let out a quiet sigh before she nodded, stepping out of the way for Bishop David to come in.

"Thank you...Mary." He said, soon walking into her home, looking around.

Mary shut the door behind Bishop David, walking past him and sitting down on a chair in the living room, continuing what she was doing before he knocked. When Bishop David sat down across from her, he noticed that she was knitting a quilt.

"Oh...I see that you've been busy with making a quilt." Bishop David said, giving Mary a gentle smile.

"Quilts. I've been busy making quilts." She said quickly, pointing in the corner to a basket of several quilts.

Bishop David was surprised by the amount of quilts she had made. "That's quite the number of quilts Mary." He said with a small laugh after.

Mary raised her eyebrows as she continued to knit the quilt. "I've found that work is one of the few things that keeps me from thinking about the past." She said softly, not making eye contact with Bishop David.

"Oh...well...if that's what helps you find peace." He said quietly, rubbing the back of his neck before he finally decided to talk about why he wanted to talk to her. "Mary...I'm worried about you."

She heard Bishop David, stopping for a second before she continued knitting the quilt. "Why?" Mary questioned him.

"I'm concerned for you because you haven't been going to church for months." Bishop David finally said, looking at her with a worried expression. "You were always an avid church-goer when William..." He said before realizing what he said, stopping in mid-sentence.

Mary immediately looked up when Bishop David brought up William, her knitting ceasing before she let out a sigh of disbelief escape her lips. She set the quilt and knitting needle down. "Please, do not ever bring up William to me again when comparing me to then and now." Mary said, her voice trembling as she had grown an upset expression.

Bishop David had become silent as he listened to Mary finally speak to him.

"I'm no longer the Mary from then because of the events that happened, and if you want to visit me and tell me how I use to love church and that you're concerned with me not being there on Sundays, then don't even speak, you're wasting your breath." Mary said to him, her eyes staring into his intensely.

Bishop David heard everything she was saying before he let out a sigh of sympathy. "I'm sorry Mary that you're like this...I didn't come here today to chastise you about not attending church. I came here because I'm really concerned for what you've become. I want happiness for you, I want you to have that cheerful personality that everybody knew you for." He said softly, standing up from sitting, looking down at her. "Always remember Mary, we all face events in life that we don't want, but it's all a part of God's plan for something greater."

Mary just glared at him the whole time he spoke, not even acknowledging the things he said. "I would like you to leave."

Bishop David heard her request and nodded softly, walking away from where they were at and leaving the house.

She had watched him leave through the windows before she finally reached for her knitting needles and quilt, continuing to knit as she thought about what he said about God having a plan for everyone. To her, God's plan was killing William and taking away something that she loved most in the world, when she didn't have anyone else.

"Forget God." Mary said to herself quietly, having completely lost faith and love in God.

Chapter III

One stormy night soon had arrived in Lancaster County. Rain had arrived over the town and fields, the sound of sharp pellets hitting the roofs and windows of each building. The window whirled between each building, the sounds of wind wailing could be heard by anyone who was awake.

While the storm stayed present in the county, Mary was asleep in her bed, although she wasn't sleeping soundly. The red-headed woman was having a nightmare, causing her to toss back and forth in her sleep before some sort of sound interrupted her slumber.

KNOCK KNOCK KNOCK

Mary sat right up from her bed like a vampire in a coffin, rubbing her eyes. "What on Earth?" She said to herself, looking around the room as she wondered what caused her to wake up.

KNOCK KNOCK KNOCK

This time, the red-head heard the solution to the noise. "Who could be at my door in the middle of the night?" Mary got out of her bed, wrapping her blanket around herself to cover her nightgown. She made her way down the stairs of her home before seeing the front door. Once she got to the door, she slowly opened it, seeing who it was.

There was a man, about her age, with a young daughter about six-years-old. They were wet from head to toe, shivering as they looked at Mary.

"Please...do you have room in your home for my child and I? We come from far away to Lancaster County...we have no home, no food." The man said, his tone being a desperate one.

Mary had no idea that this was what waited for her on the other side of the door. "I...Well..." She looked at the two before she finally nodded quickly, stepping out of the way.

"Oh thank you...thank you!" The man said happily and emotionally. He quickly moved inside, Mary shutting the door behind the two. Even though they were inside, away from the rain, they still were shivering in the dark home. Mary saw how cold they were and immediately knew what they needed.

She quickly went over to the fireplace in the living room, taking two logs that were on the side of the hearth in a pile and putting them inside the fireplace. After a few attempts of trying to get a fire started, she eventually managed to do so, an orange glow illuminating the living room.

Once the man saw the fire, he moved his daughter close to the fireplace, trying to get her as warm as possible. Mary saw what he was trying to do and quickly went over to the eight-year-old, wrapping her blanket around the child. The man soon began to dry off her daughter while at the same time trying to get her warm.

"There you go…nice and warm now. Away from the cold rain." He said quietly to his daughter, holding her close as he sat in front of the fireplace with her.

The daughter shivered still, but the warmth from the fire and the blanket caused the shivering to decrease as the time went by.

Mary stood behind the two, watching them and making sure that they were okay. "Are you warm enough?" She asked them, having held one of the quilts she had made in her hands to give to the man.

"Yes…thank you kind miss." He said quietly, holding his daughter close before taking the quilt from Mary, wrapping it around himself.

With the two warming themselves up from the fire, Mary decided to grab another quilt for herself before sitting down on her couch. She wrapped the quilt around her body so she could be warm too. Since she now had two "guests" in her home, she didn't want to go upstairs, back to bed, with the knowledge that two strangers were downstairs in her home, two people who she had no idea who they were.

"Maybe they're thieves," Mary thought to herself, studying the two strangers. *"Although…she looks pretty young to be a thief."* She finally decided to speak up, wanting to figure out who they were. "Where did you two come from?"

The man looked back at her, hearing her question before he began to reply to her. "We came from Somerset County." The man answered, still trying to warm up his daughter.

"Oh...that's far from here." Mary replied, sitting down on her couch, looking at the man.

"It very much is..." The man nodded, looking at her. "Do you know if there's any housing here in Lancaster County?"

Mary heard her question before she shrugged. "I'm not too sure. Are you looking for a place to stay?"

The man nodded, looking down at his daughter. She had fallen into slumber and had a warm expression on her face and had stopped shivering, indicating she was no longer freezing. "Yes."

She heard him and asked some more questions in order to get to know him. "Why Lancaster County? I'm sure there's plenty of other settlements along the way."

"I just," The man began to say, rubbing the back of his neck nervously, "I don't know...I guess I've heard a lot of great things about Lancaster. Figured that it would be a great place for my daughter to grow up in."

Mary nodded when he stated that it'd be a good place for his daughter to grow up in. "Lancaster really is a nice place to grow up in...a good place to start a fam-" she began to say before stopping when she was about to say "family." It reminded her of what she has always wanted to have and that made her think of William and her. "Well, it's a good place to meet nice and caring people."

The man saw her reaction when she was talking about family, but decided not to question it in order to remain polite. "That's good to hear...by the way," the man began to say, looking at her once again, "what is your name?"

She heard him and replied softly. "Mary...my name is Mary Lee Warner."

When the man heard her, he smiled softly. "That's a beautiful name."

Mary smiled softly when he complimented her name. "What about you? What's your name?"

"Robert." He said quietly, before looking down at his daughter, gently stroking her hair. "The little one is Miriam."

Chapter IV

The next morning had arrived, the rain was now gone, the only trace of rain being the puddles in the dirt. Mary decided to help Robert and Miriam out by going down to the church to see Bishop David could help them out.

Entering the church, there were only a few people present in the pews, praying to the Lord about whatever comes to their attention. Bishop David was not preaching, considering it was a Tuesday, so chances were he was at his home.

"Doesn't look like he's here." Mary said, turning around and leading Robert and Miriam out.

"Who are we looking for exactly?" Robert said, holding his daughter's hand as they walked towards Bishop David's house.

"We're looking for David, Lancaster County's bishop. He might be able to help you out with moving here." Mary replied, reaching the bishop's house before knocking on the door. Not too long after the knock, the door opened, Bishop David standing there.

"Mary?" He said, a little surprised. "What brings you here today?"

Mary explained the whole story to him, telling the bishop that Robert and Miriam showed up in the middle of the night, needing a place to stay and that they wanted to move to Lancaster.

"I see..." Bishop David said quietly, scratching his beard as he thought about it. "Unfortunately, there isn't any houses available right now."

Mary heard the news and let out a quiet groan. "So where will they stay if they don't have a home?"

Bishop David heard her before looking at the two, looking at Mary again. "Can I talk to you privately Mary?"

Mary was confused as to why, but nodded as she stepped inside the bishop's house. "What did you want to talk to me about?"

Bishop David looked at her before he let out a quiet sigh. "I wanted to talk to you privately about where they're going to stay. I believe they should continue living at your house until a new house can be built here in the county."

She listened to what he said before hearing his statement about the two staying at her home. "What? No. I can't have people living at my house."

Bishop David gave her a confused look. "Why not? You have one of the biggest houses here in Lancaster County. You're not living with anyone. There's plenty of room in the house for someone."

"Because, I don't have enough food to feed two more people. I don't want to start housing people." Mary was quick to say, folding her arms. "I can't let strangers come into my home and make themselves acquainted to the hou-"

"Mary." Bishop David interrupted, clearly showing he was getting irritated with her. "Enough with the excuses. I'm not going to force you to let them in. I'm only suggesting you give the two of them a home. It's not permanent, but where else are they going to go?" He asked Mary, looking at her with a serious expression. "They can't move into anyone else's home. They all have families, rather large ones too."

She listened to him, looking into his eyes as she thought about everything he was saying. Bishop David was right in many ways. Most families in the county had large families, homes that were already crowded. With Mary's house, it was just her. He even said that it wasn't permanent, so it'd be something that Mary didn't have to deal with for too long.

"I guess...I could have them stay for a little while." Mary finally admitted, realizing that she could be a little generous.

"Thank you Mary." Bishop David said before leading her back outside, now facing Robert. "We will discuss adding a house whenever I meet my colleagues. Until we can get a house added to the county, you'll have to stay with Mary for the time being."

Robert listened to what Bishop David said, nodding softly. "Okay, thank you."

Bishop David smiled softly, heading back into the house before closing the door.

Robert and Miriam turned toward Mary, looking at her. "So...are we going to back to the nice lady's house?" Miriam asked her father.

Mary heard her and couldn't help but smile. "Yes...yes you are."

Robert watched the two interact before he couldn't help but smile, seeing this stranger being so nice to his daughter.

"Alright. Let's head back to the house so I can get a room prepped up for you two." Mary said, clapping her hands together when she knew what she needed to do.

Chapter V

A couple of months passed by in Mary's household. The two strangers that had showed up on her doorstep were now friends of hers, having brightened up the household little by little. As Mary got to know Robert, he started feeling more and more comfortable around him, the two even joking around with each other.

With Miriam, she started to look up towards Mary as a mother figure, every now and then the little girl called Mary mom. Mary would hear this and laugh, finding it humorous that Robert's daughter called her mom.

While everyone was getting along just fine, Mary started to remember William again, every time she looked at Robert. There was something about Robert that reminded her of William. It might've been the way he made her laugh or the way he showed kindness to people. Whatever it was, Mary could see William through Robert, which made her think about if she found another William in her life.

It was now 6 PM and Robert and Miriam had finished eating dinner with Mary. When they finished, Robert decided to take Miriam to bed, since she started dozing off during dinner. Once she was in bed, she was out cold.

"She must've been really tired today. Miriam never goes to bed this early." Robert said, walking back into the kitchen. "I don't blame her...she didn't sleep that well last night."

"Oh poor thing." Mary said, cleaning the dishes in the sink. "I hope she rests well tonight."

"She probably will." Robert said, walking over before leaning against the counter. "So...what do you want to do?"

Mary continued to wash the dishes before she stopped, soon looking at him. "What do you mean?"

"Well I mean...Miriam is in bed early. Do you want to go out for a walk?" Robert replied, looking at her and waiting to hear an answer.

She looked at him before looking down at the dishes, thinking about his offer before setting the plates down. "I would enjoy that."

He smiled brightly before he walked out of the kitchen, planning on getting his jacket.

———

It didn't take long before the two were on an adventure, walking around the county in the early evening. The sky was an vibrant orange, the sun easing itself behind the hills.

"Wow...that's a beautiful sunset." Robert said softly, looking at it.

"It sure is." Mary said quietly, looking at it before she looked at Robert. With the two of them having grown closer, she soon started to think more in regards of making their relationship a bit more than friends. "Can I show you something?"

Robert heard her, turning his head and looking at her before he smiled softly. "Yeah of course."

Mary smiled brightly before leading him into the woods, walking in a certain direction. As for Robert, he wasn't sure where she was taking him, which made him a little nervous. Eventually, the two arrived in a rather large open area in the woods, a grass area that was decorated with wildflowers.

"Wow..." Robert quietly said to himself, stepping forward and starting to walk towards the flowers. "They're beautiful."

Mary stood behind Robert, watching his response before walking with him again. "I know. I love coming to this place. It reminds me of so many happy memories." She said before she began to lay down in the grass, looking at the sky that had become as orange as a Doris Longwing Butterfly's wing.

Robert watched what she did before he followed her actions, lying next to her as the two watched the sky. "You have quite the spot...especially one that you value." He smiled softly, relaxing on the grass.

The two watched the sky for a few, enjoying the time to relax with each other. Eventually, Robert spoke up, a question that had been resonating within him.

"How come you didn't want to let us live with you a few months ago?" He quietly said, still looking at the sky, some clouds gently moving along in the sky.

Mary heard him and gave him a confused look. "What do you mean?"

"You were talking to Bishop David the morning after the rainstorm. You told him that you didn't want anyone staying at the house because you didn't have enough food and didn't want housing people. Part of me though doesn't believe that."

Mary listened to what Robert was saying, her expression staying confused before her expression became more of a look of hesitant.

"There's something more than not enough food and not wanting to house people huh? You don't have to tell me, but just know I'm here if you want to talk." Robert said quietly, wanting to assure that she could trust him.

She listened to what he said before she began biting her own lip, thinking to herself before she let out a quiet sigh. "There is...there's a lot more to it. I think it's fair that you should know."

He heard her response to his question and turned onto his side, looking at her now as she began to speak about what the reason for not wanting anyone to live with her.

"It all has to do with a man I loved...a man named William." Mary said quietly.

Chapter VI

William Bradshire...a carpenter of Lancaster County. Most of the county knew him as the kind man who cared about everyone around him, even the ones who didn't care for him. William was the prime example of what it means to follow Christ's footsteps. He showed a strong love towards God, helped out around his community, showed love towards everyone, taught the youth about the Bible, and that's just the peak of the iceberg.

Sometimes in life though, bad things can occur that change one's life. For William, it was losing his parents at the age of eighteen. With his parents gone, he now owned the house, but that meant nothing to William. For a long time, he had struggled with the fact that his parents were gone, but during this time, he still continued to help people, having put them first before himself.

A great example of William putting others first was one cold, dark night. There was a knock on his door, the knock having echoed the entire silent household. When William opened his front door, he found a shivering girl his age, looking up at him. This girl was Mary.

The young girl had ran away from home, angry at her parents and her peers around her community. She was looking for a place to stay, which was she ended up on William's doorstep, a stranger to him. William was caring enough to immediately let her in; he even allowed her to stay as long as she needed. Even though she could've left any time, she found herself a priceless friendship.

Eventually, as time progressed, the redhead soon fell in love with William, the same happening with the boy. The two ended up revealing their love for each other when they discovered and rested in the grass area in the woods with the wildflowers. Ever since then, they were two peas in a pod.

As time progressed, they became closer and closer, almost being one soul. Mary began helping out in the community with him while developing a strong love of God since William introduced her to Him. Eventually, William decided that he was going to ask Mary for her hand in marriage, but his colleagues asked for his help in finishing the construction of a barn.

Unfortunately, William never had the chance to pop the question due to the accident. While he was watching his colleagues raise one of the barn walls up by pulling it up with ropes, the ropes snapped and the wall soon fell on William, his chances of escaping the wall very low with how fast the whole situation took. Sadly, William didn't survive the heavy barn wall crushing him.

Word soon got out around the county about William dying from the accident, which Mary soon heard about. She was devastated, crushed, her heart torn into pieces for the loss of her one true love.

After William had passed, Mary was given the house, considering she basically lived there and was a member of the community. During this time, Mary closed herself off from the rest of the world, locking herself away in her home, mourning the loss of William. She even decided to not let anyone into the house after the loss in order to keep the house peaceful, like it was when William and her were in it.

Even in the present, Mary still has nightmares about the whole incident, nightmares that remind her of the loss of William.

"If only I were there to stop him...to get him out of the way...If only I were there...he'd still be alive."

Chapter VII

Once Mary finished telling Robert the story, she had developed some tears from the memory of William's death.

"Now you know why I don't let anyone into the house...I know...it sounds insane, for the girlfriend of someone who has departed to keep the house like a temple. You must think I'm crazy..." Mary said quietly, wiping her tears.

"Oh no..." Robert said, looking at her. "I don't think you're insane at all...I can see why you value the house so much. All the memories with William...the laughter...the peace...everything about it...you don't want anyone to ruin this place for you." He said softly, gently resting his hand on hers. "I'm sorry...I didn't know this was the reason why you didn't want us here."

Mary heard him and finally broke down, tears rolling down her cheeks as she covered her face with her hands, muffled crying heard behind it. Robert reached for her and wrapped his arms around her, holding her close as he embraced her.

"Shhh...it's okay...Mary." Robert quietly said, stroking her hair gently to calm her down. "It's okay..."

After years of suppressing the memories of William and her, the pain she has endured from remembering his death, the many tears she had held back, she finally broke down and let her tears flow.

"I miss him so much...every day I wish I could see him again...tell him that I wish I could've saved him from the wall...I wish I could've done something." She said, pressing her face against Robert's shoulder as she shook from her crying.

"You couldn't do anything Mary...you had no idea that would happen..." Robert said softly, continuing to hold her close as she cried against him. "Look on the bright side...with William having a strong love for God, he's finally in Heaven where he can be with God...walk along with him...talk to him...laugh with him."

With Robert's words entering Mary's ears, it made her cry more. He was right in the sense that she wouldn't have known and that he's in a better place now. Her heart ached as she recalled all the memories of William from when they met to his death. All the memories were mainly happy and ones that would make her laugh whenever she looked back to them. Even though William was gone, she remembered one thing...William lives on through her. The memories, the house, the ideology, everything that William was made up of lives on through Mary. With this thought, she felt like she could finally get over the tragedy of losing William and achieve peace.

"Thank you...Robert...Thank you." Mary said quietly, looking up at him with tears in her eyes.

Robert looked down at her, confused as to why she was telling him thank you. "For what?" He laughed gently, wiping the tears away from her eyes.

"For saying all of those things about William and I...I've spent all these years holding onto William's tragedy and blaming myself for not being able to help him, but now I can finally find peace and let go of the tragedy...thank you...Robert." She finally said, looking at him as she gently reached up, stroking his cheek before she finally decided to lean in, kissing him gently.

Robert was caught off guard with the kiss, his eyebrows raising as she held her in his arms. Eventually, she broke the kiss, resting her head on his should. "Let's go back home...it's getting late." Mary said quietly, her eyes now closed.

Even though Robert had thought about pushing their relationship to another level, there was something that was holding him from reaching that level, something that had followed him from his previous home.

Chapter VIII

Many weeks had passed by since Mary told Robert about her past. Mary was in a much brighter mood, slowly building herself up again by socializing with people, going to church again, which made Bishop David happy, and she started wearing colorful clothes again.

Robert was thinking about what Mary had done in the wildflower area in the woods on the porch. He wanted to moved towards the next step, but the past was catching up with him.

"Hey!" Mary called out, coming up to the house with Miriam. "We've got dinner!"

He snapped back into reality, smiling gently when he saw the two. "Oh...that's wonderful. Looks delicious." Robert said, standing up and helping them take the food inside the house.

"I decided to cook something special for you...to thank you for helping me return back to my old self again."

Robert smiled and chuckled nervously, rubbing the back of his neck. "Oh...you don't have to do that."

"But papa," Miriam spoke out, looking at him, "look at the food! It looks delicious! At least let mom...Mary cook it for me."

Both Robert and Mary laughed at Miriam's comment, Mary picking her up and holding her.

"Okay, well if Robert doesn't want his special dinner, then I'll cook it for you." She said, walking in with the child.

"That'd be fantastic!" Miriam exclaimed happily.

Robert followed behind the two with the groceries, his expression being lost in thought as he thought about the past.

———————

Dinner time soon arrived, everyone now seated at the table as they waited for Mary to come in with the special dinner.

"Whatever she's cooking, it smells delicious." Miriam said, excited to eat.

In a matter of minutes, Mary came out with a cooked turkey, the skin being a golden crisp.

Even though Robert wasn't asking for a special dinner, he was impressed with how the turkey came out. "Wow, looks really good Mary."

She smiled brightly, setting the plate down. "Well I'm glad you like it so much. I've got more coming out. I cooked some corn, made so mashed potatoes, have some greens." Mary explained to them as she walked back into the kitchen.

It took a few trips for her before she finally could sit down at the table with the two. "Alright, dig in." Mary said, taking her knife and fork, cutting into the turkey and scooping up a little bit of everything.

The dinner that they had all together was nice. Lots of laughter, lots of compliments, complete joy filled the room between Miriam and Mary, although Robert was most of the time quiet. After dinner, Miriam decided to go play with her doll in the living room while Mary and Robert were in the kitchen, cleaning the dishes.

While they were in there, Robert remained quiet, lost in his thoughts as he kept trying to shake it off. It didn't take too long though for Mary to see something was bothering him.

"You've been awfully quiet this evening...is there something wrong?" Mary asked him, continuing to wash the dishes.

"No." Robert said vaguely, not wanting to get into what was bothering him.

"You sure?" She said softly, looking at him. "You seem like you're thinking really hard about something."

"Don't worry about it." Robert said to her, trying to avoid explaining his thoughts.

Eventually, Mary let out a quiet sigh before setting her dish down, turning toward Robert.

"You know if something is troubling you, you can te-" Mary began to say to him.

"Drop it." Robert said harshly, looking at her for a few quick seconds before he finally set his plate down, shaking his head. "Just forget it...I'm going to bed." He said, leaving the kitchen and walking upstairs.

Mary was shocked by the way Robert reacted, considering it wasn't normal for Robert to be this way.

Miriam heard the commotion from the living room, looking at Mary. "Is papa upset about something?" She said with a concerned voice.

Mary heard Miriam and shook her head. "Don't worry about it dear. He just needs some time to himself."

Chapter IX

Robert currently laid in Mary's bed upstairs, his eyes closed as he tried sleeping. He didn't mean to snap at Mary, but considering his thoughts were getting to him, it was bound to happen. As he attempted to sleep, he soon felt something lay next to him, which interrupted his slumber. He opened his eyes and turned to look and see if it was Mary.

Of course, he was right in this situation. Mary was in her nightgown, having crawled in bed with Robert, getting cozy. Once he saw it was Mary, he returned back to his previous position, his back facing her. Still trying to avoid breaking the news to Mary, he soon felt her arms around his stomach, her body soon pressing against his back.

"What's going on with you? You're usually not like this." She said softly, resting her head against his back.

"I don't know Mary...I don't know." Robert said quietly, his eyes still closed.

"I feel like you do know Robert." Mary finally said. "I just feel like you don't want to tell me what you're thinking of."

He heard what she said, but didn't reply to it. The only thing he did was sit in silence with his eyes closed, trying to fall into slumber.

"You know I'm here if you want to tell me what's bothering you. I think it'd be healthy if you did though because you won't get any sleep with you thinking about whatever you're thinking. I know from experience." Mary quietly said, now closing her eyes as she rested her head against his back.

Robert listened to what she was saying before he let out a quiet sigh, trying to think about how he would explain his thoughts to her. Eventually, he decided to be straightforward with her.

"You know why I decided to move to Lancaster County?" He asked Mary quietly.

She merely shook her head against his back, indicating that she didn't know why he moved here. "Aside from finding a new home, no I don't."

Robert listened to what she had to say before he continued. "I left my previous home because my wife walked out on Miriam and I."

When Mary heard this, her eyes opened up and she sat up, looking down at him. "What? That's horrible! Why would she do that?"

Once Mary sat up, Robert turned so that he was laying on his back, now looking up at her. "To be honest...maybe I married the wrong person. She just...everything seemed fine to me. She was a good mother, I was a good father, we lived a happy life, but then one day..." He said before stopping, thinking back to that day before telling Mary what happened.

"Sara?" He called out, looking around his home. "Where are you?

While he walked around the house, Miriam watched him, not understanding what was going on. "Papa? What's going on?"

"I can't find mom. She's gone." Robert said, his tone being a little more scared. "Maybe she left something saying where she went. Yeah...she leaves notes."

"Maybe...I'll help you try and find something" Miriam said, getting off of the couch before walking around their home, trying find anything that could lead to the mystery of where Robert's wife went.

Eventually, Miriam found a note that had fallen on the side of the bed. "Papa!" She called out. "I found a note!"

Robert immediately ran into the room, seeing the note in Miriam's hand. He took the note from her and began reading it. Although the hope he had on his expression when he found the note soon faded the more he continued to read it. In fact, he soon had become emotionless from what was written on the note.

"What does it say papa?" Miriam asked, looking up at him.

Robert finished reading the note, looking down at Miriam before folding the note in half, tucking it into his pocket. "Don't worry about it sweetheart. I think though...we need to move away from this county."

When Miriam heard this, she was completely confused. "Why? Why do we need to move?"

He heard her before he picked her up, looking around the house one last time. "Because I think we will find somewhere else that'll be better for the both of us."

———————

"We basically left the county with nothing but the clothes on our back. I couldn't stand living in the same county as her and live in a house that we lived in together." Robert said quietly, looking at Mary as he finished explaining his story. "Would you stay in the same place if you found out your love left you and your child for someone else?"

When Mary heard this, she let out a depressed sigh. "No...I don't think I would." She said quietly. "Is that what's been on your mind today?"

Robert heard her before nodding softly. "I've been thinking about it for a long time now...I've wanted to move onto the next step in our relationship, but...I fear that something would happen again...I fear the odds of you walking out on us."

Once Robert said that, Mary spoke up in a more serious tone. "Robert...look at me."

Robert did as told and look into her eyes, seeing what she would say.

"I would never do that...ever in my life." Mary said, looking at him as she gently rested her hand on his cheek. "I wouldn't do something to hurt you and Miriam...I love you both, with all my heart." She said to him before she gently kissed him, breaking it soon after before resting her head on his chest. "You don't need to worry about me every walking out on you two...I care about you two so much that my heart aches. I wouldn't even think about walking out on you two."

When Robert heard this, he let out a relieved sigh, his arms wrapping around her and hugging her against him. "I love you so much Mary..."

"I love you too Robert..."

THE END

The Painted Lake

ABBY BARKER

Emma hadn't missed a sunrise since she was old enough to help Mama with the laundry, with the exception of that day last winter when she woke up with a cold that kept her bedridden. To Emma, the sun peeking over grassy horizon signified the beginning of all things: life, journeys, and the potential that comes with each new day. Waking up after sunrise would be like turning down a message of encouragement from God, which Emma couldn't bear to waste, so she woke every day at the crack of dawn ready to face whatever challenges arose and accept all graces given to her. This was a schedule that she intended to keep for all time.

This morning, though, she almost missed it. The night before she spent tossing around in her bed, sometimes staring at the ceiling, sometimes the wall, but almost never the backs of her own eyelids. She was restless, but careful to move softly as not to wake up her pig-tailed younger sister, Abigail, who would not have to feel this nervousness for another handful of years, if she would even feel it then. If it was up to Emma, she would have been baptized years ago, but Mama insisted that she take some time to "test her faith." But she already knew her faith to be true; in her heart she knew it. That was enough for her, why wasn't it enough for Mama? This was the last thought she had before finally drifting off to sleep just before dawn.

It seemed as if no time had passed when Abigail gently nudged her sister awake just as the sun began its morning assent.

"Emma! Em!" she half-whispered, "It's today. You've got to get ready. You've got to go so you can hurry up and get back to tell me everything! What do you think Auntie Willa is like? You have to drive a car!"

Emma couldn't match her sister's excitement, but Abigail was right about one thing: The sooner she left, the sooner the month in the city she and Mama had agreed on would be over and she could come home.

"Abigail, please!" she snapped, "I hardly got any sleep and I have plenty of time to pack my bag." She wouldn't have to pack much. In her letters, Auntie Willa insisted they would go shopping the moment she got settled in.

"The clothing is part of the experience," wrote Auntie Willa, "you won't need your bonnet in the city!"

Emma frowned as she rolled away from her sister and turned her back on the dawn. She wanted to stay in bed forever, but she'd settle for five more minutes.

***

After completing her morning chores, Emma changed into a simple, but flattering white linen dress she thought was suitable for traveling. She looked at herself in the mirror as she brushed her long, sun-streaked hair, trying to untangle the knots on her head and in her stomach. A furrowed brow shaded her wide, hazel eyes and her dusty pink lips were downturned in a nervous frown. Each stroke of the brush brought her a little comfort, but not much. There was a lot to be nervous about. She had never met Auntie Willa and they had only spoken through letters. Mama, while she couldn't contact Auntie Willa herself, suggested that Emma reach out before she left on rumspringa. If she had to leave her home, Emma thought, she might as well try to stay with a family member while she's away. Even if that family member left on rumspringa herself 19 years ago and was the only one of her friends not to return home.

Since Emma wasn't yet an official member of the church, she was allowed to write to her excommunicated aunt, but she did so begrudgingly and only at her mother's expressed wishes. Emma could tell that Mama missed her sister, which helped assuage her reluctance to reach out. If Mama still cared for her, she couldn't be all bad. Even so, that first letter was tough for Emma to write. It read:

Dear Auntie Willa,

We've never met before but Mama says you're her sister, which makes you my aunt. She says you used to look just like her, but your hair was always wilder. I have many aunts and uncles here at home, but you're the only one who lives in the city. Mama said it would be a good idea to write you even though you're not with the church anymore because I'm eighteen and she wants me to see the English world before I'm baptized. If I had it my way, I'd already be baptized by now but Mama thinks it's important to face temptation, and deny it, before I make my decision. If I already know there's nothing that could tempt me more than the Will of God, why should I bother with rumspringa? You're probably not the right person to ask.

Your niece,

Emma Byler

Emma was surprised by how kind Auntie Willa seemed in her reply. She told Emma how excited she was to hear from her oldest niece and that she missed the family "something fierce." She also said that she agreed with Mama that seeing how the other half lives, especially if Emma was going to choose to stay with the church, was incredibly important. The way she said "if" put Emma on edge, but she couldn't help but like her aunt after reading the rest of the letter. Auntie Willa wrote enthusiastically and earnestly, offering up personal details about herself (she had an apartment in Chicago with a collie-mix named Charlie), and ended almost every other sentence with an exclamation point. Eventually, Auntie Willa asked Emma to come stay with her for a while.

Emma instinctively put the brush back on the vanity in front of her before remembering the open suitcase next to her. She picked the brush back up and packed it away. Auntie Willa was already on her way. She offered to drive down from Chicago to pick Emma up since no one in her family owned a car, and their horse and buggy wouldn't be able to make the journey to the city. In her letters, Auntie Willa kept referring to it as a "road trip" in an attempt to make the long ride sound more fun, but Emma had never been farther from home than the next town over and the idea of sitting in a car, another thing she had never done, for hours on end was daunting. Just as she zipped up her bag she heard the sound of Auntie Willa's car pulling up to the house. She sat on her bed with the bag in her lap for a few minutes before meeting her aunt in person for the first time.

When Emma finally walked into her family's kitchen, Auntie Willa was sitting at the table with a cup of water that Abigail brought her. She was wearing a bright red t-shirt tucked into a bright, floral-print skirt that brushed her ankles. Her curly, chestnut hair had apparently never lost it's wildness, but was clipped back in a twist that made it look like the strands were trying to escape. She and Emma had the same eyes, which were staring happily at her from across the room. Mama couldn't see any of this while she stood at the sink washing dishes and her back turned to Auntie Willa.

"Emma!" she yelled, jumping out of her chair and almost knocking over the water, "Emma, I'm so frickin' excited to finally see your pretty face!"

Mama bristled and Abigail stifled a laugh at Auntie Willa's objectionable language. Emma just stood stock-still as Auntie Willa rounded the kitchen table, arms outstretched like a bird taking flight, and encircled her in an enthusiastic hug.

"Emma, we're going to have so much fun. I mean, of course you're going to be doing some very valuable thinking and learning, too," she shot a careful glance at her sister, "but that doesn't mean it won't also be tons of fun!"

This made Mama briskly dry her hands on her apron, step away from the sink and pivot towards the hugging pair.

"Now you listen, Willa. Emma is staying with you because I think it's a necessary part of a young person's life to look the world straight in the eyes, knowing everything they need to know about their choice, and say 'My priorities lie with God.' It's not about fun. It's about free choice and true faithfulness. I know you clearly don't see it that way considering the path you've chosen, but Emma isn't like you, Willa. She's steadfast and faithful and knows exactly what she's doing."

Auntie Willa was taken aback, but her arm never left Emma's shoulders.

"Jodie, please. I took this decision just as seriously as you did. I just used me 'free choice' a different way is all. I'm sorry that meant things had to turn out the way they did, but it was my choice. Just like this will be Emma's. So if Emma wants to have fun, we're gonna have fun! And if she doesn't, well, what are the odds of that?"

She gave Emma a subtle wink and playful jab at her side, knocking her a little off balance. She regained her footing and spoke up the newly found courage that having her aunt's support provided.

"If it were up to me I wouldn't even be going. Mama, you asked me to do this, so I'm going to do it, but you can't ask me not to have fun. You have to trust me to do the right thing. I don't plan on doing anything in Chicago that I wouldn't do here."

Auntie Willa scoffed gently at this.

"Sweetie, I wouldn't say that. Even riding the elevator up to my apartment is going to be something you wouldn't do here, but I get what you're saying. You and your mother both can rest assured knowing that I would never make you do something you weren't up for. Cross my heart."

She made an "X" in the air over her chest with her right index finger, but Mama didn't look convinced with her arms crossed over her own chest.

"You have to trust me to do the right thing," Emma interjected through the tension.

"Sweetheart, of course I trust you." Mama walked over to her daughter and embraced her. "I know it doesn't seem like it at the moment, but I'm proud of you and grateful that you're doing this. God will guide you. As long as you follow your heart and His word you'll make it through."

She kissed Emma on the top of her head and reluctantly let her go.

"I love you Emma."

"I love you too, Mama. Don't worry about me. I'll make the most of it."

Emma then walked over to her sister and gave her a hug goodbye while she chattered away about clothes, boys, and Navy Pier. She tried to soak up as much of Abigail's excitement as she could before picking up her bag and walking out the door. Mama and Abigail followed them out to the car. When she saw the vehicle, Abigail let out an excited scream and ran over to it.

"It's red!" she yelled back at Mama and Emma, as if she thought they couldn't see it yet. Emma approached more cautiously. It seemed safe enough, by the looks of it, but she knew it could move ten times as fast as any buggy. She imagined the car being pulled along by two of her family's horses and allowed herself a small smile. Auntie Willa offered to help Emma with her bag just as she got close enough to run her fingers along the cool, smooth surface of the car. The trunk popped open on it's own and made Emma jump. Auntie Willa dangled the keys in front of Emma's surprised face.

"Cool, huh?" she said with a grin. Emma only smiled back and nodded. "Well, it's time to hit the road. If you forgot anything we can just pick it up when we get into the city. Bye, Abigail! Bye, Jodie! I'll try to get her back here in one piece!"

Auntie Willa opened the passenger side door for Emma and she slipped inside. She watched her aunt walk around the car to her own side and hop in, flashing Emma a faux-nervous smile. Emma watched her aunt pull the seatbelt around her body and clip it into the buckle. She took the cue and, after a little bit of fumbling, was safely buckled in. Auntie Willa put the key in the ignition and the car started with a low roar.

"You ready, Em? No turning back now!"

Emma didn't know if she was ready, but she knew she had to be.

"Yes, Auntie Willa. Let's go."

"That's the spirit!" Auntie Willa replied joyously as she pressed a button next to her to open the front two windows. "Wave to your mom and sister. They're gonna miss you!"

Emma stuck her hand out the open window and looked back at her family standing outside. Abigail could barely contain herself as she fidgeted from foot to foot waving frantically. Mama was her opposite, standing tall and still, neither happy nor unhappy about seeing her oldest daughter drive away to Chicago. Emma pulled her hand back inside just as the car began to move. Her stomach lurched, but the feeling receded the farther they drove from home. Auntie Willa turned on the radio and started humming along. Emma kept her eyes locked on the road in front of them, watching her neighbor's homes fly by out of the corner of her eye. Auntie Willa's words echoed in her mind. *No turning back now!* She was tempted to turn around to see what her house looked like from this far away, but she took those words literally. There will be time to turn around later, she reminded herself, but this was the beginning of a new journey and she was determined to face it head on.

***

The view outside Emma's window slowly morphed from just ripened soy and cornfields to suburban neighborhoods filled with cookie cutter homes and chain grocery stores. She spent the first hour or so of the drive silently watching the world around her change and she felt herself changing, just a little bit, with it. From the safety of the car she was slowly immersed in this new world and allowed herself to become accustomed to it, but she didn't know what to expect when she stepped out.

Auntie Willa had been mostly silent up until now. She happily sang to herself and understood that Emma was the type to quietly take things in before wanting to talk about them, but Auntie Willa was not that type and after an hour of quiet she had about reached her breaking point.

"Are you getting excited? I remember sitting on the edge of my seat about to burst when I left home for the first time."

"I guess I'm...surprised? I thought it would be harder to leave than it was. I thought things would feel more alien, but after passing through all of these towns that look the same it's starting to feel familiar. Does that make sense?"

'Totally! I was blown away by the first Target I saw, but by the ninth or tenth it definitely lost its mystery. Don't you worry, though, Chicago is gonna knock your socks off. I've lived there for almost two decades now and it still takes my breath away when I'm driving toward that skyline. I'm definitely gonna take you to the planetarium. You won't get a better view of the city, or the universe, from anywhere else. I swear, it'll change your life."

She agreed to go on this trip to reassure herself and her family that she wanted her life to stay the same. She hadn't given any thought to how she might come home changed. This thought both scared and excited Emma. For the first time, she allowed herself to think of the experience not just as a trial, but also as an adventure.

"I think I'd like that. Back at home the sky is filled with millions of stars at night. After dinner Abigail and I sometimes go out into the yard and lie down to look up at them. I know that most of them already have names, but we'd lie there and come up with names of our own. I usually picked names of people from the Bible. It's comforting to think God's people are looking down on us, but Abigail always named the stars after boys she likes," Emma giggled at the memory and Auntie Willa followed suit.

"You won't see many stars in Chicago. The sky's mostly filled with planes and helicopters, but you'll be able to see all sorts of things at the planetarium. All the stars named after your sister's crushes and then some!"

Emma tried to imagine how they got all the stars to fit inside one building when the entire skyline of Chicago rose up out of the rode in front of her. She'd never seen it before but she knew it couldn't be anything else. Auntie Willa glanced over at Emma and saw her eyes grow wide.

"Awesome, isn't it? Just you wait."

This feeling was not what Emma expected. She wanted to know what it felt like to be amongst those buildings, and all the people who live in them. She wanted to know how it felt to be a part of something so massive and seemingly intangible. The buildings look small on the horizon, but Emma was still struck by their size. She was so caught up imagining how it would feel to sit on top of the tallest building in Chicago and see the landscape change backward from city, to suburb, to home that she almost forgot she'd planned to go back.

***

Auntie Willa had prepped her for the elevator, but she still gripped the railing with white knuckles when it began its assent. Auntie Willa lived on the nineteenth floor of a high-rise with two bedrooms and a sweeping view of Lake Michigan. One bedroom was Auntie Willa's and Charlie had unofficially occupied the other until the day before. He was a little put out when Auntie Willa dragged his bed and toys out into the living room, but immediately changed his tune when he met Emma. She didn't even have a chance to realize that she'd never been this high up before Charlie bombarded her with doggy kisses. Emma's family didn't own any official pets, just their horses and some chickens, but she immediately warmed up to him.

"Charlie likes you! I knew he would," cooed Auntie Willa.

"I like him, too! We've never had a dog," Emma replied, scratching Charlie behind the ears.

"Well you do now. Mi perro es tu perro!"

"What?"

"Oh that's just a little Spanish for you. It means 'my dog is your dog.' I can teach you a little while you're here if you'd like."

Emma didn't know that Auntie Willa could speak another language. She was impressed by how worldly her aunt was, but then remembered that focusing her attention on things like that is what drew Auntie Willa away from the church in the first place.

"Maybe, but I don't know what good Spanish would do me back home."

It was clear Auntie Willa didn't agree, but she refrained from pushing the matter.

"Why don't you get settled in your room? Maybe hang up some of the clothes you brought, take a shower, and I'll order up some Chinese food. You ever have Chinese food? Probably not, but you'll love it. I swear!"

"Okay," was all Emma could muster. She had only ever eaten what Mama or their neighbors had cooked for her. The idea of "ordering" food was as unfamiliar as "Chinese," but she was uncomfortable denying Auntie Willa's hospitality. She took her bag into the spare room and began to unpack before cautiously figuring out how to work the shower.

When she got out of the bathroom she found a warm looking pair of sweatpants and a baggy t-shirt waiting for her on her bed.

"I know you probably brought a nightgown with you," Auntie Willa yelled from the living room, "but trust me, there's nothing cozier than a hand-me-down pair of sweatpants that are too big for you."

Not one to protest, she pulled on the black pair of pants and the shirt that said "Chicago Marathon 2013" on the front and met Auntie Willa in the living room where a feast of little white boxes, black plastic containers, and a mountain of fortune cookies was waiting for her.

"I didn't know what you liked so I got a little bit of everything. Plus, I told them we were having a party so they'd give me extra fortune cookies. Dig in!" She handed Emma a plate, a pair of chopsticks, and a fork just in case.

Between surprisingly delicious bites of fried rice and sesame chicken, Emma asked her aunt about the t-shirt.

"Did you run a marathon, Auntie Willa?"

"Ha! I just bought ten pounds of Chinese food. What do you think? No, my ex-boyfriend gave me that shirt while we were dating."

Emma was suddenly uncomfortable about the idea of wearing a man's shirt, and Auntie Willa could see that.

"Don't worry, girly, he hasn't warn that shirt in years so it practically never belonged to him in the first place."

This reassured Emma enough that she continued to wear the shirt but now she had more questions.

"Auntie Willa, how many boyfriends have you had?"

"Well that depends. I've officially had three serious boyfriends, but I've casually dated quite a few more."

This took Emma aback. Mama met Papa at a Sunday evening sing and that was that. The girls at home almost always end up marrying the first boy who takes them home in his buggy. The idea that Auntie Willa had dated more than one man, had even worn their clothes, shocked her. She wondered how many other men's t-shirts she had in her closet, but she didn't dare ask.

"Wow," she replied, "I've never even held hands with a boy."

Auntie Willa chuckled kindly, "Well let's see what we can do about that, huh?"

This made Emma blush wildly and spoon too much rice into her mouth to keep from having to respond.

***

Auntie Willa wasted no time fulfilling her promise to take Emma to the planetarium. The very next day, after gently insisting that Emma borrow some more of her clothes and that she "leave the bonnet at home, girly!" they hopped in a cab and made their way to the museum.

The Adler Planetarium sat out on its own at the tip of a peninsula that jutted way out into Lake Michigan. Driving towards the impressive domed building gave Emma the same sensation as when she first saw the Chicago skyline. She couldn't wait to get inside to see where they kept all the stars, but after the cab dropped them off at the entrance Auntie Willa put her hand on Emma's shoulder to stop her from immediately sprinting up the stairs to the front doors.

"Hold up! Turn around first. Don't you want to see what I was talking about?"

Emma turned and saw the same skyline that awed her from a distance magnified and close enough to touch. That impressive massiveness that she felt fifty miles away was now right on top of her. The beautiful weight of the city was balanced on her small shoulders and she loved it. This feeling was enough to cause a small chip in Emma's resolve to return home, and this frightened her. She spun around on her heal, as if not being able to see the skyline made it not exist. She wasted no time climbing the stairs to the planetarium now. She relied on the familiarity of the stars to remind her of why she wanted to go home, but she didn't count on what else she would find inside.

***

After wandering around the exhibits for a while, taking in every fact about space, the stars, and especially the Sun that she could find, Auntie Willa suggested that they sit for a while and see a show. They decided on one called *Skywatch Live!* which showed how the night sky above Chicago would look if the city turned off all of its lights. This one interested Emma the most. She wanted to see how different the sky is here as opposed to at home.

Soon after they took their seats in the huge, domed theater the lights dimmed and the starry Chicago sky was projected above them. Emma had to stifle a gasp as every star she'd ever seen and more swirled above them. She was loath to admit it to herself, but it was almost more magical than the real night sky at home. Wrapped up in the tableau unfurling in front of her, she was caught off guard when a voice projected across the audience.

"Welcome, everybody! Thanks for coming out to see *Skywatch Live!* with me. My name's Nathan, and I'll be your night sky tour guide today."

Nathan had a pleasant voice, confident but not too rough. Emma thought he sounded like he had a sense of humor that he wasn't quite ready to share with the audience yet. Then she thought she shouldn't be thinking about this strange man's voice at all and tried her best to focus on the stars.

"Later on tonight, you'll probably be able to see Saturn even with all of the city lights. Do you want to hear a bad joke about Saturn?" A smattering of people in the audience cheered him on. "Okay, don't hate me for this. Why does Saturn have rings?"

"Why?" the audience, including Auntie Willa, happily asked.

"Because God liked it so he put a ring on it! Saturn is not a single lady."

He was met with a mixture of laughter and groans from the audience. Emma didn't really understand the joke but she found herself laughing anyways. There was something about the way Nathan said his joke was bad that made her feel like he actually thought the opposite. She could tell by his voice that he amused himself and she couldn't help but feel endeared by that.

"I told you it was terrible! Let's move on. I'm embarrassed," Nathan continued, but Emma knew he wasn't.

Emma tried as she might to focus on the show but Nathan's voice kept drawing her in. She wanted to know more things about him; what he looked like, if he liked Chinese food, did he want to hold her hand. Her cheeks flushed at that thought. He didn't even know she was in the same room as him, let alone if he'd be interested in *that*. More than that, she didn't even know who he was really, just the sound of his voice. Just as she began to talk herself out of these feelings for Nathan, he concluded the show and told everyone to come see him if they had any questions about the show. This chance to talk to him face-to-face squashed all of the doubts in her mind as she scrambled to think of a question.

"Auntie Willa, I've got a question for Nathan. Do you mind if we stop and ask?"

Auntie Willa had a hunch about Emma's true intentions.

"Sure thing. I actually have to use the ladies' so how about we meet by the sun when you're through?"

"Great, thanks!" Emma replied before speeding away full of nervous energy.

Emma tried to slow down to give herself time to think of the perfect question but before she knew it she was standing in front of a tall brunette man with a kind face and a nametag that said "Nathan."

"Hey!" he greeted her, "Did you enjoy the show? Gotta question for me?"

Emma nodded and asked the first thing that came into her mind, "Why was your joke funny?"

Nathan was not expecting this question, but he hid his surprise behind an understanding smile.

"The joke about Saturn? It was a reference to a Beyonce song where she talks about some guy who wouldn't marry her. So, I guess the joke's funny for that reason, but also can you imagine God marrying a planet?" This made him laugh, but only confused Emma.

"Who's Beyonce?"

"Who's Beyonce? What are you, an alien?" he replied incredulously, but not unkindly.

Emma picked up on his playfulness and said, "No, at least I don't think so. I grew up out in the country where there isn't much music except for in church. I guess that might as well be another planet compared to here."

It turned out more than just his own jokes could make Nathan laugh. He let out a whoop and wasn't shy about it or his feelings.

'I like you!" he said, "What's your name?"

"Emma," she replied, her signature blush swept across he face, but the traditional shyness that usually came along with it wasn't there. In fact, she had never felt more confident. Against all odds, and especially against her own rules for herself, she liked him too. She felt a small pang of worry about what consequences she might face for these feelings, but she pushed them away at least for this moment.

Nathan stuck his hand out in front of him and said, "Nice to meet you, Emma. You already know my name, but would you like to know more about me?"

"Absolutely," she said as she excitedly shook his hand. This was the first thing she felt confident of since she got here. It was only after giving Nathan Auntie Willa's phone number that she realized they had held hands, and in that moment she felt more alive than any day she had back home. Emma was in love and terrified.

***

Emma didn't have to wait long by the phone before Nathan called. She and Auntie Willa talked about him that night after they got home from the planetarium. She was excited for Emma, but warned her not to get her hopes to high about some guy she just met. Emma wanted to explain that he was more than that, but didn't know how to put it into words. She was having a hard time understanding these feelings herself. Luckily, Auntie Willa was a young girl in love once, too, and understood that sometimes these things need to run their course.

"Hey! Is this Emma from the planetarium?"

Emma had made sure that Auntie Willa gave her a complete lesson on how to use the phone well before she actually had to answer it.

"It is! Is this Nathan, also from the planetarium?"

"Sure is. Now let me get straight to the point, because I'm sure you've heard enough of my disembodied voice. I want to take you to dinner. Do you eat on your planet?"

Emma couldn't help but giggle girlishly.

"Yes, of course we eat!"

"Perfect. I'll come by your place around six. I'm thinking it's about time you tried classic Chicago deep dish pizza."

"We definitely don't have that where I'm from, but it sounds great!"

"See you then, then. Buh-bye Emma."

"Goodbye!"

Emma couldn't believe what she was about to do. In her wildest dreams back home she never thought she would be going on a date with a man in the city, let alone enjoy it. Auntie Willa was right.

Chicago was changing her and it was starting to become difficult not to think it's for the better.

***

Nathan took Emma on a handful more dates over the next few weeks before they finally came back to the planetarium. In that time she had learned his favorite color (red), how many siblings he had (two), his favorite book (*A Brief History of Time*), and he learned all that and more about her (sky blue, one, The Bible). But she couldn't help but feel that he was keeping something from her. He was almost unnervingly forthright with her, to the point where she felt like she could ask him anything, but when she asked why he worked at the planetarium he grew solemn. This only lasted a moment before he coolly replied, "because I love teaching people about space!" but she could tell that wasn't the real answer. It made her uncomfortable that she knew there was something Nathan was actively keeping from her, but she was so happily in love that she didn't want to push him away by prying.

At the planetarium, Nathan had arranged a private, after hours tour for the two of them. This was the first time she had been alone with him and that made her nervous, but excited. Nathan had been nothing but a gentleman to her the entire time they were dating. He could tell she had some reservations about becoming physical with him, and he respected that. They often held hands in the park and always hugged goodbye when he dropped her off at home, but had yet to kiss. He knew about her religion and the fact that she was only here for a couple more weeks, but every time she anxiously brought up the fact that their relationship had an expiration date he just held her close and told her not to worry about anything but that exact moment. Each time he held her, Emma could never see the sad smile Nathan had on his face.

They made the same rounds through the exhibits as Emma and Auntie Willa did the first time she came here, but this time there was no one else around and Nathan told her secrets about different artifacts on display. She loved every second of it, but couldn't help wondering about the one secret that he wouldn't share with her.

Eventually they made their way to the same theater where they first met. A starry sky was projected above them and on the floor at the front of the theater Nathan had arranged a romantic picnic, complete with different cheese, candles, and a bottle of champagne. Emma was so overwhelmed at the sight of this gesture that she kissed him right there in the doorway. She hadn't planned to, but her nervousness slipped out of her body the moment Nathan's lips touched hers. They were as soft as down, but the pressure he put behind them made it seem like they might never part. Nathan softly grabbed the back of Emma's neck with one hand and held her waist with the other. She instinctively wrapped her arms around his neck and pulled his body as close to hers as she could without fusing them together.

This kiss was like seeing the city for the first time. It was like the first bite of Chinese food. It was lying on the grass looking at the stars. It was sunrise.

When they finally parted she could see that Nathan was silently crying.

"Nathan! What's wrong? Should I not have done that?"

"No!" he said chuckling through the tears, "You definitely should have done that." He sighed and touched her cheek. "I've got to tell you something. Will you sit down with me?"

Emma felt a knot in her stomach as Nathan lead her to the blanket surrounded by candles. He popped open the champagne, poured them both a glass, and said, "You're beautiful."

"Is that what you had to tell me?"

"It's one thing, but it's not *the* thing."

The way he said *"the* thing" made it sound like some sort of storybook monster.

"Just tell me. You're making me nervous."

"Emma... I'm dying. Like, really, incurably, probably quickly dying."

Emma couldn't say anything. At first, she thought this was just another of his bad jokes but it became clear by the tears welling in his eyes that he was serious. She threw herself into his lap and cried with him, spilling the champagne onto the blanket. They held each other quietly for a while before Emma finally spoke.

"I love you."

"I love you, too"

In that moment nothing else mattered to Emma. Her home, her family, God were all forgotten as she lay there on the floor with this surprising man that wasn't even supposed to be a part of her life. Now he felt like a permanent fixture. That night she decided she could ask for forgiveness later. They had found somehow each other in an infinite universe and that was a gift more precious and unique than any other. They made love in the theater that night under the stars.

***

Emma stayed in the city just long enough to go to Nathan's funeral. She wore a simple black dress that Auntie Willa lent her. The funeral was held in a Catholic church filled with ornamentation, extravagant robes, and subdued singing. She couldn't help but feel that Nathan would have wanted something simpler, more light hearted, but who was she to say? Her first love had come and gone like a comet. She broke her own rules, as well as God's and had nothing left to show for it. When the priest called everyone up to take communion, Emma just shook her head and cried. He understood, said a blessing over her, and sent her back to her seat. She didn't understand the tradition, but felt oddly comforted by it.

When she got back to Auntie Willa's she couldn't talk at all. Emma went straight to bed and shut the door. Tomorrow she was supposed to return home. She lay awake in bed for hours thinking about if that's what she really wanted after all. Around five in the morning she gave up trying to sleep and started to pack. She left the blinds open that night and soon her room was filled with pink and orange light. The sun rising over Lake Michigan painted the sky and made the water look like light. She watched the top of the sun peek over the horizon and slowly fill the sky. "This is a new beginning," she reminded herself, "Not just for me, but for Nathan, too."

The sight of something so familiar, but all together new gave Emma the answers she needed. Looking out over the painted lake, she knew she would be okay.

END

BEAUTIFUL UNUSUAL

ELOISE EDWARDS

Colette awoke suddenly. Her pale skin was even paler, and dripping in a cold sweat. It was not the first time this nightmare had woken her in the middle of the night. Of late, she had been plagued by the thought of her eldest daughter Abigail, and her aversion to marriage. The oldest of three girls, Abigail was the only one to remain unmarried. Her choices had caused her mother many sleepless nights. She was fast becoming the only woman of her age without a husband. Colette wanted nothing more than all of her daughters to settle down and find a man that could care for them, to bring up children of their own.

So far, Abigail's siblings had found just that. Bridget had married her school mate and long time friend, John. They had made the arrangements the previous year and were now in their own home with their precious young son. Earlier this year the youngest of the three girls had also married, Jessica was now moving from her family home and into the house her and her husband had built. That just left Colette and Abigail. Almost every night since the wedding of her youngest daughter, Colette had tossed and turned in her cotton sheets, picturing her eldest child, an old spinster with no one to care for her and no children of her own. She could not bare the thought.

Her worst fears were quickly becoming a reality. Abigail was by all means not interested in any of the men within the community. Her only love was her love of teaching. Many an argument between the two women had ended the same way. Colette was always cautious when broaching the subject, although she knew what the end result would be.

"I just saw young George from your class at school, he is looking very handsome these days," She would hint. Colette would stare back at her eldest and await her dishevelled response.

"Mother, please. We have been through this so many times before," Abigail's nostrils flared in anger and her cascade of straight, brown locks would float around her waist. Colette looked on as her rage built up.

"I am not interested in seeing any men. All I want right now is to concentrate on my teachings. You know how much this means to me, why will you not respect that?" She raged. Her slender hands slammed down flat against the kitchen table in front of her. The wooden surface shook with the force of her displeasure. Colette was the first to back down. There was no way to change her only unmarried child's mind. She could just pray for her to one day find happiness with a partner she could depend on.

Abigail had become comfortable with her adult life in the childhood home. Since she was born these walls were the only ones that she ever found comfort and safety within. She had been there through every prominent event that had occurred in her life. It was full of her memories, good and bad all the same. Through her study to become a teacher. Through her fathers death. They had rejoiced and mourned within the confines of these walls. However, as her siblings left, she found it feeling that much more empty. She missed waking up to her sister's laughs from down the hall. Now there was just her and her mother.

Each morning Colette watched her daughter leave for her job and each evening she returned exhausted from the lengthy day that had just passed. Colette just did not understand the fulfilment she found at work, having never had a job of her own. In the end, she just wanted her daughter to be happy, she just assumed that her happiness would be in the comfort of a loving relationship with her true love.

One fall, her day had begun as usual. She mapped out the teaching plan for the day and rounded up the children to come to class.

"Time for school now, kids!" She called out the the playground. One by one they made their way inside and the teaching started. All the children loved her and enjoyed coming to class each day. She was so engaging and it was evident that she enjoyed every moment of her job. They read stories and learnt arithmetic. She worked on handwriting with them and taught them most importantly about the Amish faith and the rules of the community that they were born into.

The day ended all too quickly.

"Okay, kids its time to go home now, pack up your things and we will wait outside for your parents to arrive," She called. She watched as all of her students rushed back to their desks and cleaned up before making their way back out of the front door to wait for their respective relatives.

One by one they were taken home. Mothers, fathers, grandparents and aunties came. They thanked Abigail for her time and took their children back home for the day. Last was William. Abigail had been friends with his mother, Josephine, since they were just children. They had been quite close, until she married her now husband. Once she was pregnant they drifted apart somewhat. Their lives had taken them in different directions. Never the less, they remained friends. She saw Josie almost everyday when she arrived to get her first and only son from Abigail's class. But today, she was not alone and Abigail did not recognise that man that she brought with her.

Before she had a chance to ask, Josephine introduced the stranger to her.

"This is my brother," She said. Abigail remembered from long ago that Josie had a brother. When they were young he had left for Rumspringa and never returned. She barely recognised him.

As Josephine's brother entered the wooden door frame her heart seemed to skip a beat. He was by far the most handsome man she had ever encountered in the flesh. His hair was bleached blonde from the rays of the sun, giving his short locks a golden tinge. Dark to light, the blonde streaks danced across his head of hair, falling into a sculpture of wavy strands. His skin was darker than his sister's, tanned deeply by his lengthy stay in the outdoors. His figure was absolutely perfect in her eyes, with muscular toned limbs peeking from the rolled up sleeves of his white, collared shirt. He donned long pants but she could still make out the muscles in his long legs beneath. He looked down at her and extended a rough hand for her to shake,

"Nice to meet you, I'm Kane," He greeted her politely. Abigail felt her cheeks begin to blush, she held a hand to her face to attempt to mask her fluster and delicately placed her free hand in his.

"Abigail," She stuttered. Never had she felt this way before, and needless to say it had overwhelmed her. This outsider had swept her off her feet and they had barely spoken a word. Was this what love felt like? She wondered. No. Surely this was just the excitement and lust that consume you when coming across a foreign man. She had never met anyone from outside of the community and so this feeling may be something else entirely.

"So, you are the teacher here I assume, Josie has told me a lot about you." He continued. Again she felt her body overwhelmed with embarrassment. Her modest living had not allowed for compliments of unfamiliar men. The conversation continued awkwardly until the sun began to set and the brother and sister pair were forced to leave so that she could lock up the old school house. As they made their way with young William down the front steps they waved goodbye to Abigail,

"I hope to see you again soon," Kane winked at her. Abigail gathered herself and mustered a reply,

"Me too." In an instant they had disappeared and the large wooden down swung closed behind her. She lay with her back against the smooth door and sighed. Never in a million years had she thought that she would feel this way about a man, but her mother was right. Maybe she was meant to wed. But would her mother truly be pleased if she brought home a stranger to their way of life? No matter if he was related to Josie, a woman she had known since they were just children. Alas, she was jumping ahead of herself again.

Abigail gathered her belongings and locked the school house behind her. She merrily skipped home to her mother. For the first time in a long time she felt genuinely happy.

As soon as she stepped in the door, Colette noticed her change in demeanour. She waited until she sat down at the table to ask,

"You look happy tonight," She commented. Abigail smiled sheepishly.

"I just had a really nice day at work today, mother," She replied. There was no way she was going to admit the real reason she was so chipper. Colette sighed inwardly. Her eldest daughter did not care for anything but her job and today was apparently no different. They ate dinner and chatted about their dealings during the daylight hours before heading off to their respective rooms for the night.

As soon as Abigail's eyes closed for the night she was taken back to her meeting with the handsome stranger she had encountered that day. Kane was the star of her dreams and for once she had not a care in the world for her work. He was just happy to be in his presence, even if it was only in her dreams.

The next few days flew by. Abigail found herself haphazardly teaching her class, with one eye resting on the window hoping for a glimpse of Kane. Every so often she would catch from the corner of her eye a figure, but it was never him. However, that afternoon Josie sent him to pick up her precious son. He was one of the last to arrive before Abigail locked up for the evening. He rushed up the steps to meet his nephew.

"Hey William, how was school today?" He questioned. William smiled up at him, delighted to see his Uncle here to pick him up and bring him home.

"It was fun!" He exclaimed. He picked up his tiny knapsack and ran down the stairs.

"I hope he wasn't too much trouble," Kane said to Abigail as she grabbed her keys and locked the door behind her.

"Not at all," She replied. William was one of her better behaved students after all, he was never a hassle. Kane smiled at her and her heart jumped around in her chest once more. She had never felt anything like this before.

"I am glad, he is a pretty good kid. One day I hope I have a child like him, if I'm lucky," He laughed. They watched as he made his way to pick up the knapsack by his feet.

"I was wondering," Kane began,

"Would you perhaps like to go on a picnic or something this weekend?" His voice became shaky, like he was overcome by nervousness all of a sudden. This was the moment that Abigail had been dreaming of for some time now. She thought for a moment before wording her reply,

"I would love to," She replied. They organised a time and place to meet, then he grabbed William's hand and they proceeded to walk back down the stairs.

"See you this weekend," He said as he waved her goodbye and made his way down the dirt road toward home. Finally, her dreams were becoming reality! Never had she thought that he would be interested in someone like her, but she had been proven wrong. Quickly locking the doors, she ran home to her mother to let her in on the exciting news.

"I can not believe it!" Colette exclaimed once she heard the news. She was sure that her daughter would never allow herself the opportunity to love, not after the arguments they had had on the subject. But finally, she had found someone. Regardless of his standing within the community, she could not hide her joy. She prayed that he was the one for Abigail. She would settle down and birth grandchildren. They spoke for hours on the subject. The sun had set long ago and they realised that it was past midnight.

"Goodnight," Colette said as she left for her bedroom. She could rest easy that night, knowing that her eldest was no longer adverse to love. It had taken much longer than any of her other children, but the day she had been hoping for had finally arrived, when she had least expected it. She had found someone finally. Abigail could rest easy too, looking forward to the weekend that was to come.

The end of the week arrived in a flash. Soon it was Saturday morning and Abigail was busy getting ready for her first ever date. She had not courted any man before so this was all new to her. She picked out a modest dress and donned her bonnet for the outing.

She made her way out of the front door, saying goodbye to her mother as she left. Kane was just walking up the dirt road as she closed the door behind her.

"You look beautiful," He cooed. She blushed immediately, lifting her hands to her face to cover her obvious embarrassment. He took her hand and led her to the clearing he had picked out for their date. He let her go and pulled a large blanket from his backpack, laying it on the ground flat. He patted a spot, beaconing her to sit as he dug around for the food her had prepared. Abigail's jaw dropped as he brought out sandwiches, salads, cakes and vegetables.

"Did you make all of this?" She asked. He nodded and placed a chicken sandwich on a plate, offering it to her. It was the most amazing day. They talked and laughed and filled up on the spread of food Kane had prepared. They bathed in the warmth of the sunlight shining down on them. There was no where else she would rather be than here. They connected on so many levels. It did not matter that he was no longer belonging to the Amish community she had always known. He was the only man that made her feel this way. Even after one date she knew that she had fallen madly in love with the person before her.

As the sun began to set, they packed up and he took her back home. He held her hand all the way up to the door of her house. She grasped the handle and opened it wide.

"I had a great time today," She said. Kane agreed.

"We will do this again soon," He assured her. He felt exactly the same way. Despite his years away, he did not share this connection with anyone until he had met Abigail. They said their goodbyes and she disappeared into the house. Colette was waiting patiently for her to get back.

"How was your picnic?" She questioned excitedly.

"Just magical," Abigail replied. There was nothing in the world that could ruin this for her. Or so she thought.

Abigail and Kane met on and off in the days that followed. Each meeting strengthened the bond that they had formed. She could not imagine life without him, and him without her. They were falling deeply in love with each other. It seemed as if nothing could go wrong.

Weeks later, while Abigail was teaching and Colette was doing the daily chores, a strange woman made her way to their front door. She was dressed in modern clothes and drew the attention of their neighbours and friends as she approached. She quickly pulled a hand-written note from her pocket and slipped it beneath the front door before turning to leave.

Abigail was the first to arrive home that day. As she opened the door she stepped on the note that the woman had left. Puzzled, she bent down to pick it up.

She began to read the note. The words on the page made her hands shake. It read;

'Abigail,

I have seen that you have been with my ex-boyfriend, Kane. I know that from the outside he seems harmless but being with him will cause more harm to you than good. Meet me on the outskirts of the corn fields at midnight tonight and I will explain in person what I mean by this. I do not want him to hurt anyone again. I could not bear the thought of letting him do this again.'

What could she possibly mean? That night Abigail debated in her head whether or not she should go to meet this person. She trusted Kane so much, but it dawned on her that she knew nothing of his life outside of the community. She had to know what this was about.

She made dinner with her mother and they sat down to eat together.

"How was your day?" Colette asked over the table as they ate. Abigail responded with a general 'fine'. There was no way she would tell her mother about the mysterious note that had been left for her. She would never approve of her leaving so late at night to meet a stranger with no name. The night continued as usual. They finished dinner and cleaned the table. Abigail washed the dishes and placed them away in the cupboards above her head.

The two women sat down in front of the fire before finally it was time for bed.

After they had both said goodnight, Abigail waited in her room until the clock struck midnight. She crept out as the bell sounded, it drowned out the sound of her footsteps and the door closing behind her. No one was on the street and a blanket of darkness covered her as she made her way to the meeting point. As she approached, she could see the shadowy figure of a woman standing there. Cautiously, she made her way to the edge of the field.

"Hello?" She whispered. The woman turned to face her. Her long, blonde hair hung delicately by her shoulders and her short skirt showed graced the tops of her thighs. It was an outfit like Abigail had never seen before. She was definitely from outside the community.

"Hi, Abigail is it?" She reached out a hand to shake.

"Yes, who are you?" Abigail longed to get straight to the point. The woman took a deep breath before she replied,

"My name is Kaitlin," She said. Kane had never mentioned Kaitlin to her before.

"Would you like to sit?" She asked. Abigail shook her head. She just wanted to know what was going on.

"I came because I can not sit by and watch him take advantage of anyone else," Kaitlin blurted out. Then came the story of how they had broken up.

"He took everything from me. I was with him for years and one night he just disappeared and left me with no money, I could not even make the rent." She began.

It turned out that Kane had met Kaitlin on Rumspringa all those years ago. It was her that had tempted him to stay out in the modern world. They had been happy for several years, until one day Kane had disappeared. But, he had not just left with him belongings. He had taken all of Kaitlin's savings, leaving her with nothing.

Abigail was in shock. Surely, the Kane that she knew was not the same as the man Kaitlin was speaking of. But everything lined up. The time that he had come back was the same as when Kaitlin had been robbed and left high and dry in the city. She felt sick to her stomach as Kaitlin's words continued. Abigail's face drained of color.

"Are you okay?" Kaitlin asked. Abigail did not answer. Had everything just been a lie? Di he really love her, or did he just want access to her savings so he could leave, just like he did with Kaitlin? Questions flooded her head. Before Kaitlin was done, Abigail turned and ran back home. She could hear Kaitlin calling from a distance.

"Wait!" She begged, but Abigail kept running. She found herself back home and headed to the comfort of her room. She did not sleep for the rest of the night but lay there, awake and wondering if what Kaitlin had told her was true. She needed to know and there was only one person who could confirm her story. She dreaded to ask Kane, but she knew that she must. It was the only way to put her mind at ease.

The morning sunlight beamed through the window. Abigail got out of bed, not having slept a wink all night. She quickly got dressed and made her way over to Josie's house, before her mother had even awoken. Her nerves overwhelmed her as she made the walk to her destination. As she knocked, Josie answered the door instantly.

"Hey, Abby. How are you this morning?" She smiled. Immediately she saw the look of worry on her friends face. There was something wrong.

"Can I see Kane, if he is in?" She asked.

"Certainly," Josie replied and she led Abigail through the kitchen and to the backyard where Kane was busy chopping firewood. He looked up at her and a smile spread across his face.

"Abigail, I was coming to see you as soon as I was done with the firewood!" He said. She approached him and sat on the cool grass, covered in morning dew. She beaconed for him to join her. He put down the axe he had been wielding and sat by her side, he could sense that something was wrong now.

"I met with a girl called Kaitlin last night,"She began. She turned to face Kane and saw that his face had dropped. She relayed the information Kaitlin revealed the previous evening, the stealing and lying she had accused him of.

"Is it true?" Abigail asked, hoping desperately for his denial of the whole thing.

"It is," He sighed. She felt tears welling up in the corner of her eyes. How could this sweet and compassionate man be capable of this? He continued,

"I can explain," But before he had time to finish his sentence, Abigail stood up and made her way to the street.

"I do not know what to think about this, Kane. I need some time to think." He pleaded with her not to leave but his attempts were futile.

"Please, wait," He called. But she was already gone.

She slammed the front door of her home as she entered, alerting her mother of her return. Colette rushed to her daughters side, she saw the look of distress on her face and asked her what on earth had happened. Abigail broke down and told her everything. All about the ex-girlfriend she had et the night before and how Kane had cheated her out of the money she had saved up for them. He had returned he shorty after to start again.

"What if he takes everything I have too?" She sobbed. She had never thought she would be in love and now hers was in jeopardy. Colette's face showed her obvious remorse for her daughters troubles. Still, there was a chance that he was a changed man.

"Has he ever given you a reason not to trust him?" Colette questioned. Abigail shook her head. Even when faced with the horrible accusations by Kaitlin, he had told the truth to her. He could have easily denied the happenings for the sake of her love, but his honesty had prevailed.

"He has always been honest with me. I truly believe that he cares." She expressed. Now it was up to her. Could he change for her? She definitely needed some time to think about things. Abigail and Colette agreed that some time apart from Kane would be best to figure out the next step she would take and whether it was worth the risk.

He came to her house everyday after that. Colette answered the door and told him that she was out when in truth Abigail watched the conversations from her bedroom window. He pleaded with her mother to let him visit her. He wanted to explain that these circumstances he found himself with Kaitlin had been a lapse in judgement. He would never do that to Abigail. He was truly in love. Despite his pleas, Colette turned him away each time.

"She needs some time to think," Colette stated before shutting the door with him on the other side.

One day, after class, Abigail was left with just William, waiting patiently for Josie to arrive. Since their disagreement, Josie had always picked William up, trying desperately to make this situation easier for both her brother and her friend. The teacher and student chatted while they waited for his guardian to come and retrieve him at the end of the day. But alas, it was Kane who made his way up the road and toward the old school house.

Abigail's jaw dropped as she stared at the man she had been avoiding for weeks. This time she had no where to hide, no one to save her.

"Hello," He said as he made his way toward his nephew.

"Good afternoon," She stammered. Even with all this time apart her heart still skipped a beat when she saw his handsome face staring back at her. She longed to give him a chance to explain himself but all rational fibres in her body told her otherwise. Still, her heart begged to be in his arms once more.

William skipped down the school steps,

"Bye Miss!" He waved to her.

"See you tomorrow, William," She smiled. Before she knew what was happening, Kane had her hand in his.

"Please, can I see you tomorrow afternoon? After class. I need to explain what happened between Kaitlin and I. It was extremely complicated and I am not the same person as I was back then. You have changed me Abigail. I want to be a better man because of you." He pleaded with her. Tears welled up in her eyes once more. It was time to hear him out.

"Sure," She responded. She had no idea what kind of explanation he could come up with to make this right, but she prayed that it was good enough to take him back. She wanted desperately to be with him, get married, have children and start a new life together. She wanted to get past this. She watched as he walked away. Despite her worry, she could not wait to see him again the next day.

When she got home she revealed the days events to her mother.

"What should I do?" She asked. Colette thought for several minutes before replying.

"I think you should hear what he has to say." She responded. Abigail ran over and gave her a hug. She had not been sure until this moment that she was making the right choice. But the reassurance from her mother confirmed her feelings. She had to try.

That night she tossed and turned. Her mind was working overtime, throwing questions back and forth around her brain. Would his excuse be good enough for her to be with him? Could he really change from the person he was before? Would he end up leaving her like he did Kaitlin? She searched for answers but she could find none. The morning came all too quickly.

Exhausted, Abigail got out of bed and began her morning ritual, worrying excessively about the afternoons events to come. She dressed in her modest gown and placed the bonnet on her head. She looked herself up and down in the mirror as she tied the bow beneath her chin. She slipped her shoes on her feet and made her way down the stairs to the kitchen where her mother was already preparing breakfast for the two of them.

"Did you sleep alright?" Colette asked as her daughter entered the kitchen. The bags beneath her eyes gave the answer. Abigail shook her head as she sat down at the table and began to eat the oatmeal her mother placed in a bowl before her. Lazily, she made her way out of the house and to the school house, greeting the children as they arrived for the day. Their parents thanked her for her time as they dropped the children in one by one. Her class slowly filled and as the nine o'clock bell rang they took their seats and it was time to start class.

The lessons flew by. The children were happy as always and Abigail found comfort in their carefree demeanour. They went through their times tables and worked on handwriting until the evening when it was almost time to leave once more. The afternoon rolled around all too quickly. She watched as their parents arrived in groups to pick up their brood. Hand in hand they left. She watched as the people of the community made their way down the old, dirt road. Once again the kids left to their respective houses, leaving just her and William once more.

"Uncle Kane is coming to get me today," He stated happily. Regardless of what was happening between the two of them, William truly adored his uncle.

"That is very exciting for you," Abigail smiled at him. She loved how happy Kane had made William. Ever since he had come back she had noticed such a positive change in him. He was happier and doing much better academically in school. Surely, this could not be the result of the man Kaitlin had described to her on that night many moons ago. The two of them waited for what seemed like ages for Kane to arrive. Eventually they saw the male figure making his way up the road before them.

He held a bunch of freshly picked flowers in his hand as he walked toward the two of them. Her heart leapt in her chest as she watched him approach. Eventually he was just feet away from at the base of the steps.

"Hello, Abigail," He greeted her politely. He reached out to her and offered the flowers,

"I thought you may like these," This time it was Kane who blushed profusely. She grasped the flowers from his hand and thanked him. William jumped up and gave him a hug around the waist. Kane rustled his hair with a rough hand and sent him on his way. He knelt down to William's height and said,

"Why don't you start walking little man, I need to talk to your teacher for a second. I will watch you don't worry, okay?" William nodded happily and waved goodbye to Abigail as he started his journey home. Kane took a seat on the steps next to Abigail and they sat in silence for a moment.

"Look, there is nothing I can really say, I did take that money. I am ashamed of what I did and how much it hurt Kaitlin. Our relationship had been rocky for sometime and I wanted desperately to get home. I had no where else to go and I thought that if I took the money I could get back and get a job so that I could replace it for her and start again. Since you left me, I have gotten together what I could and started to make amends with her. I have nearly paid her back now."

Abigail looked up at him. She had not thought about why he had taken the cash, only that it had been detrimental to his ex-girlfriend and she struggled once he was gone. Maybe this relationship was not broken beyond repair. Perhaps there was hope after all.

"So, has she forgiven you?" She questioned. Her big eyes glazed over. She held her breath as she waited for his response.

"She has begun to, I did the wrong thing by her and made her life difficult. But now that we have spoken she has started to understand the difficult position I was in emotionally. She knows that what I did was not to spite her... I did love her once, but since that love faded I longed to be back with my family. And once I met you, I finally know what love truly is." He leaned toward her and pressed his soft lips against hers. She closed her eyes tightly. This was her first kiss and it was better than she had ever imagined. In the isolation of the empty school house their kiss continued on for what felt like forever. As they parted she knew in her heart that she loved him too.

"I am begging you to give me another chance," He said softly, holding her chin in his hand. He gazed into her eyes. She thought about his proposal, did she dare trust him again?

What about what Kaitlin had divulged to her? Did she dare trust him? The same questions had tortured her for weeks. They plagued her, taking over her life. They haunted her dreams which were quickly turning to nightmares. Surely if he was capable of something so horrid once he could do it again. But her heart told her another story. His remorse had shaken her to her core. Looking into his sad eyes, she knew that what he spoke was the honest truth. For herself, she needed to give him another chance.

"I am willing," She replied. She did not know if this was the right choice, but there was only one way to find out. She needed to give hi the benefit of the doubt. Weeks of silence between them was enough in her eyes to show him the error of his past ways. He had learned from his mistakes and if she did not give him the chance now there was no hope for them.

"Thank you," Tears began to stream down his face. She wrapped her arms around him and he around her as they sat in a tender embrace. It was the beginning of a relationship that would stand the test of time. Abigail knew that above anything else, she wanted a life with him. He was the only man for her.

Years later and Kane had proposed marriage to Abigail. He asked her mother Colette if he could ask for her hand, she was only to happy to oblige. The shock of it all swept her off her feet. She accepted immediately, she had never been happier. The two newly weds had the chance to settle down. They built a house to call home. By the following Spring, Abigail was heavily pregnant with their first child. They sat together on the front porch and watched the sun set over the fields. Never had she imagined this was the path her life would take, but it was true that she would not change a thing. Kane made her happier than anyone else. Her mother could finally rest easy, knowing that her daughters were safe and loved in homes of their own.

www.ingramcontent.com/pod-product-compliance
Lightning Source LLC
Chambersburg PA
CBHW022003120726
47992CB00001B/385